MW01223523

The Stag and the Horse

Horse

Chant of the Flooded #1

Fainne J. Firmin

Celestial Isles Publishing

CONTENTS

Chapter 1
The Stag Begins to Run

I COULD SMELL THE smoke before I could see it. A thick, bitter smell that coated my nose and tongue. I wondered, perhaps, if they had decided to try smoking an auroch.

But then I saw the smoke, a cloud of grey and black hanging in the air. The world around me grew hazy with every step.

I broke into a run.

The basket hanging from my shoulder bounced against my side, but I didn't care if I lost some mushrooms and herbs. My heart pounded an anxious drumbeat, though I told myself it was just a hearth fire burning a little wild. A few logs of green wood mistakenly tossed in.

Down the embankment to the river, and then along the shore, I ran until I could see our settlement.

The smoke was thick, heavy; a billowing bank that made me cough. I could see flames flickering along one of the huts, another already reduced to smoldering cinders. The worn paths, all the workspaces, were deserted.

An urgent chill filled me as I dropped my things and tried to throw dirt on the fire – it took long enough to prepare the skins and put together a frame, we had to save what we could.

1

I gave a shout, my throat burning. "Some help over here! Anyone!"

Silence. Absolute silence.

I stopped throwing dirt and looked around.

Something was wrong.

My gut twisted. "Ama?" I called out nervously, "Aita? Eider?"

Giving up on the burning hut, I hurried over to my family's home, the ground slick mud. "Ama! Aita! Please!"

The hut had collapsed, the wood frame snapped. The arch of great tusks, the last remains of the behemoths my ancestors had once fought, had buckled inwards, destroying the entrance. I screamed for my parents, for my sister, as I dragged pieces aside to get in.

I could just crawl in on my hands and knees, my fingers digging in the gaps under the frame and skins. There were still the fur blankets, and the stores of nuts and other foodstuffs. One of the baskets had overturned, spilling out the beads my mother had been making for a new hair strand.

My fingers brushed something familiar and smooth, and I shoved the structure aside, freeing it and filling the air with ash. The piece of antler was still brightly polished from many touches, the carving still clear.

My stomach twisted, throat growing closed. My father's atlatl. Passed from his father, and his father before him; no matter what happened, he never would have willingly left without this. It was a tie to ancestors, to family, to ourselves. It was carved with the same stag from which our clan took its name.

The atlatl dug into my hand as I crawled out, my stomach churning like it was going to come out of my mouth. My breath shuddered as I drew it in. What had happened? What . . .?

I staggered to my feet. It must've been sudden, they must be planning to return, they had to have left a message – I stumbled through the settlement, past more collapsed huts and spills of smoldering embers.

The ground was a sticky, muddy mess, as if it had rained, even though the sky had been bright and clear since morning. All the tracks were muddled and smeared. I passed by the clan idol, standing tall and lonely, and froze.

Sticking out from under a pile of timber and skins, was a hand.

I raced over, but the hand was cold. And tiny. I swallowed and breathed once, twice; then, because there was no one else, uncovered the body.

The little girl's stare was empty, her eyes wide. I laid her out the best I could and tried to close her eyes. She'd been unlucky, hit wrong by something falling on her.

But why had she been left here, long enough for her to grow stiff?

Leaving the little girl for now, I continued to search the settlement. It was possible someone else had also been unlucky, and that maybe they were hanging onto life.

I found two more bodies; one an elderly man behind a pile of firewood, the larger logs having crushed his leg, and another around my parent's ages, side all bloody. I couldn't tell what had caused the wound.

3

Aside from them, I couldn't find anyone. It was as if the entire clan had just vanished.

That wasn't possible, it wasn't –

My eyes landed on something in the mud.

Hoofprints. A trail of hoofprints in the mud, leading to the river.

For a moment, I didn't understand what I was seeing. The wild horses would never come this close to people. They avoided all traces of people, that's why they were hard to hunt –

The Zaldi.

It felt like the ground fell out from under me.

The Zaldi, the demon horses. We told stories of how they were sweeping in from the east, how if they reached our lands they would grab people and drag them beneath the water, drowning them and carrying their corpses to the world of demons. They were vicious, deadly.

And they'd been here.

The hoofprints, the slick mud on a sunny day, how everyone was just somehow *gone* – the Zaldi had raced through the settlement and dragged them off to another world.

The back of my throat burned, everything around me growing blurry. I gasped thickly for air, scrubbing at my eyes. They were gone. My family. My friends. They were all gone. And they weren't coming back.

The thought of never seeing them again crushed at my chest. The Zaldi had them, they couldn't even spend the afterlife in peace –

Shuddering breaths filled the air as I buried the tears. Pale dots appeared on the back of dirty hands and I clamped my jaw down. I pushed myself up from the sticky mud, hands trembling.

Falling apart now only meant joining in an unhappy afterlife. More importantly, I couldn't leave my entire clan trapped in the demon world as they were. Everyone knew that if you destroyed the demon responsible, you could free the human soul.

Something cold took root in me. It was the Zaldi who had done this, and the Zaldi who would pay the price to set my people free. I would make sure each and every one of them paid a life for a life.

My hands and feet itched, restlessness settling into my limbs. No, not yet; first I had things to do.

The House of the Dead still stood, the beams just as fresh-wood as when we'd erected it mere weeks ago. Inside was shaded and cool, the ground already softened in preparation. It was easy to use the adze and dig three new graves.

Dragging the bodies over was unpleasant, but I couldn't leave them like this, to doom their souls to wander unhappily. I did my best to place them in the correct positions and orientations.

There wasn't time to do everything, so I grabbed some of the votive figures that dwelled under the idol and set them inside the graves. I murmured words of not-quite-remember prayers. They had always seemed so easy to remember and conjure up before, when everyone else was speaking them too.

I couldn't do much more for them, aside from looping the bead strands I took off their bodies around the neck of the clan idol. Maybe it wasn't right, to encourage their souls to linger in this area, but I didn't know what else to do. Where do you guide free souls to, when their people are gone? I hoped the ancestors would treat them kindly.

It was more than I could bear, to stay in the settlement. After the fires had burned themselves out, and the last few structures had given way, and the air cleared, it had left everything feeling open and exposed and lonely.

I found a good basket I could wear on my back, and got a couple stone hand axes and scrapers, a bone knife, and a bow drill. A fire pot I tied from my waist, embers inside heating the case. With luck, I wouldn't need to use the bow drill for a while yet.

I also took a good bow and as many arrows as I could find. I bound dozens and dozens of replacement arrowheads and small blade pieces into a skin pouch; I didn't need to lose them through a gap in the basket.

I filled a waterskin from the river, just in case, and salvaged what pouches I could of nuts and berries and some spring tubers. The less I needed to hunt, to butcher and thus attract a predator, the better.

Staring at my family's atlatl in my hands, I thought about bringing a spear or two with me. They were strong weapons, but large and unsubtle. I could be quicker and stealthier with just my bow. But I wasn't leaving the atlatl behind. I tied it to my belt.

After salvaging a fur coat and a pair of hide boots – even these seemed singed and discoloured – I told myself that was it. I had what I needed, or at least everything I could reasonably carry.

Inside me, the ache in my heart as I glanced back at my ruined home – even the fields had been trampled, and I wondered where our herds had fled – was overshadowed by cold anger, an arrow of ice aimed at the Zaldi. I would not let the souls of my family, my friends, my clan, remain trapped and tormented in the world of demons.

I set the sight of my lost life behind me, and began to walk down the shore of the river, following the faint impressions of hoofprints.

I wasn't the sort of girl who spent her whole life in the settlement, cooking, sewing clothes, and weaving baskets. If I had to stay home, I was better at driving aurochs and mouflon to grazing land. When given a choice, I'd always preferred hunting and trapping and foraging, which made me very much my father's daughter, though I'd never really done any of that alone for any length of time.

Going as far as I could and back on foot in a single day was one thing, but even going to one of our hunting camps was normally a three- or four-person trip. No one ever went far alone. There were too many things that could go wrong alone.

But I was all alone.

Even if I knew where to find another clan, which I didn't, what then? Asking strangers to accompany me as I avenged my people seemed wrong. They might not even believe what I said. Worse, they could try to make me stay with them, and put it all behind me. The very thought made my insides fragment painfully.

Still, it wasn't easy to do this alone.

I kept to the river at first. Hoofprints traced its shore. An abundance of plants I could eat grew along its shores, and water wasn't a problem. Fish shimmered beneath the surface, and I realized my decision to not bring only a spear was a poor one. The river drew small game, like rabbits, at least.

The trail of hoofprints faded away quickly, but I stayed with the river. Zaldi were demons of water and dwelt in lakes. Sooner or later, the river would lead to a lake, I thought.

The trick, then, would be to lure the Zaldi to the surface. Diving for them was foolish; I couldn't kill them underwater, and if I dove too deep, I wouldn't even make it to the world of demons, for the serpents who dwelt between our worlds were sure to kill me.

The sun and moon danced in the sky, always just out of each other's reach. I didn't know what I'd do when I got to a lake, but in the end, it didn't matter, for the river grew flatter and wider until a marsh spread before me. A marsh was no place for the Zaldi, for it was too shallow, and teamed with fish and plants and herbs.

Realizing there was a marsh just a few days walk from where we'd settled for the summer would have been a blessing, but now it just left me feeling hollow.

It was too early in the season for many bugs to be out, so I slept that night, fireless, on the shores of the marsh. The stars made a familiar blanket above me. The Great Bear, the Cub, and the Hunter watched the world at night, faithful guardians of my slumber.

Ainara . . . Ainara . . .! My mother's voice whispered with the conspiratorial mirth of a prank pulled just before dawn, rousing me from sleep. I opened my eyes.

The wind whispered on, in the grass and over the water's surface. Just the wind. No voices. No mists. No ghosts.

Something hot burned in my throat, but I shoved it down and scrubbed sleep from my eyes. There was nothing here except me, some fish, and some rodents. Even the birds weren't up yet.

I ate a cold breakfast and thought on what to do next. The marsh was unlikely to turn into a lake, and I wasn't about to turn around to try following the river in the other direction. I could see the light green smudge of a forest on the horizon, sending a thrum through my nerves.

A forest would be plentiful in food, but going alone was risky. If the forest was large and I went in too far, I might wander to the world of the dead, never to return; or worse, I could draw the ire of the wolves who guard the doorways. It was certain death, to brave unknown forests alone.

For the morning, I skirted the edge of the marsh, until the looming woods gave way to rolling hills and grassy meadows full of just-colouring sedges and lumpy tussock grasses. When the wind blew, the stalks rippled like the surface of water.

It was empty, exposed, and beautiful.

It was also where we'd often find wild horses.

I didn't know where the Zaldi lingered, when they weren't in their lakes, but alongside their natural counterparts seemed like a good enough guess.

With my basket full of everything I could scrounge from the marsh, I started off across the grassland. The sky was a bright grey, the sun's arc nearly invisible. I tried to remember how many days it had been, but my mind was a haze, and the sky was too washed out to tell.

In the grassland, every direction looked alike. I picked a few stalks as I went, running them through my fingers to drop green grains into a bag. Added to some water, and it'd make a decent porridge. My elder sister, Eider, had always been good at mixing grains and herbs to come up with something tasty. I'd never quite mastered the art.

I wasn't ever going to taste her food again.

A few grains blew away on the wind. I watched them twirl and dance and scatter beyond sight. Never to be seen again.

There was a lot I'd never see again.

There was something crushing me, a dull ache, a pressure in my chest. Sometimes it was weak enough I could barely notice it. Other times it'd be like this, and I felt like I would be squeezed out of existence.

I wondered, if I let it, would it squeeze and crush until nothing remained of me, and my soul was set free to find my family and clan?

I shook my head to clear it, the wind throwing some of my hair braids into my face, ticklish streaks of brown and ochre, colours that fit this landscape of swaying grasses. I tucked them back, my bead strands clacking. The sound of them was grounding, a reminder of family, of who I was, of what it meant to be one of the Bizkor Oiloa.

The last of the Bizkor Oiloa.

If I let myself be crushed into nothingness by this feeling, then I was dooming everyone, myself included, to become wild, vengeful spirits, instead of peaceful ancestors. To become that, forever, was far worse than merely dying.

At least until I'd dealt with the Zaldi, I'd have to keep that crushing feeling at bay. I drew in a clean breath of air, felt the sharp wind on my cheeks. I couldn't keep thinking like this. I had a task to do.

Looking across the grassland with renewed purpose, I realized I'd made a fatal error. Aside from the smudge of green forest in the distance, everything looked the same, and I had forgotten to mark my path as I went. Where I'd come from and where I was going were the same.

I groaned and sat down. "Well," I said into the wind. "I guess I just wait for nightfall. At least you taught me to read the stars. . . .. I hope you're listening, aita."

I didn't hear my father's voice whisper back to me, and I wasn't sure if that was a good thing or a bad thing.

For a long while I just sat there, waiting for the hidden sun to set, and the moon to clear the sky and show the stars. It seemed to be taking a long time, far longer than it normally did. I chewed on a couple picked-to-soon berries and a mushroom. I saw birds wing in the sky and debated about risking the arrows to try and bring them down.

The ground vibrated, a faint tremor rippling along the grit. I shifted to a crouch, alert, scanning the swaying grasses. If a herd of red deer was cutting across the grassland, I could maybe take the chance of breaking one off and shooting it. They were small, so not much would go to waste, and smoking it would last me a fair while.

There was movement in the distance, a dark shadow moving across the landscape. The movement was fast. Too fast.

Horses.

I sprang to my feet, the weight of my gear creaking down onto my shoulders once more, and set out at a jog towards them. The horses moved quickly, in short bursts of impossible speed. I kept them just in sight as the day grew long and my shadow began to darken and stretch to the side.

The longer I ran, the closer the horses grew. I could see some details now. They weren't the Zaldi, just horses. I could tell by how short they were, how thick their legs were, the fluffs of manes and fur around their hooves.

I kept after them as the world around me darkened and the ground dipped down and up and down again.

In the moonlight, the horses stopped. Steam curled off their bodies as they gathered close to one another, snorting, and seemed to settle down. My eyelids were drooping; they were ordinary horses, not Zaldi, and if they left it was sure to wake me, so I dropped to the ground right there and fell asleep.

The next thing I knew, a whinny was ripping through the blue of pre-dawn, yanking me awake as the horses stamped about. I squinted into the blue, as an angry whinny echoed from the distance and hoofbeats pounded.

Shadows appeared in the gloom, familiar yet strange, throwing the horses into a panic.

The Zaldi charged into the dawn.

CHAPTER 2
THE HORSE SWIFTLY FOLLOWS

I 'D NEVER SEEN SO many horses in my life, horses and Zaldi. They thundered about in a pounding, screaming, writhing mass. I could barely make heads or tails of them and scrambled back on my hands to avoid getting caught up and trampled.

The Zaldi were so much like horses it was disturbing; but they were taller, their limbs slimmer, and they had much shorter fur. Like serpents trying to be horses.

They were demons, so that was a real possibility.

I could only watch as the two herds scuffled, and then the horses fled. The first golden beams of the day's sunlight warmed the earth, and in it the Zaldi seemed to glow.

For a few long minutes, all I could do was gaze at them. They stamped and snorted and tore up grass like normal horses. But they weren't normal horses. They were demons. Demons who'd had no problem stealing away my clan.

My hand tightened around my bow. I didn't know if these Zaldi were, specifically, the ones that had taken my people. But, I reasoned, there couldn't be *that* many Zaldi in the world, and certainly there'd be less in the general vicinity of where my clan had settled. In any case, getting rid of Zaldi could only help.

I crept forward as the world grew lighter, the sun adding a meager warmth to my limbs. There were about seven or so of the Zaldi, chomping at grass and bickering amongst themselves. Their colours were a bit off from normal horses, now that I could see better. The browns and bays were lighter, one had a reddish tinge, and one more of a yellowish ochre colour.

It wouldn't be possible to take on all the Zaldi, but I could see that up ahead the ground grew rocky and uneven, with many crevices and runs that were perfect for hunting. I'd drive some where they had no place to go, and kill them.

I gave a shout and leapt out from behind the sedges. I raced down the hill as the Zaldi neighed and crashed into one another. Most took off faster than an arrow, but two pushed against each other and stumbled.

I yelled again, throwing a rock to drive them to the right. They skittered, teeth flashing at each other. I drew an arrow and shot. It streaked and sank into Zaldi flesh, and the scream sent a fierce rush of glee through me.

The one pushed itself free and ran after the others. The injured one ran in jerky bursts. I chased after it, trying another shot and losing the arrow as it moved wildly. I drove it towards a dead-end run, the ground hard under my feet.

Rock walls loomed large and cold, and the Zaldi's hooves slid as it stopped. It danced around, voice thin and anxious, the one leg dragging. I stopped, blocking its exit, breathing heavily.

I nocked an arrow. "You shouldn't have killed my clan," I said savagely. Whatever tricks it had, whenever it tried to catch and drag me off, I would end it.

But the Zaldi never charged. It just danced back and forth, the eyes surrounded by white and rolling. I stared down the arrow shaft at it. Surely, any moment – it just wanted me to let my guard down – then it would –

The Zaldi's head drooped. Foam flecked its mouth, and a trickle of blood dripped from where the arrow pierced its flank. Perfectly ordinary red blood.

Demons didn't bleed, or if they did, it certainly wasn't going to be red. And it wasn't *acting* like an angry demon, or anything other than an – an injured –

An injured animal. That's all it was. An injured animal.

Cautiously I lowered my bow. Still, the Zaldi didn't charge me. "What have I done," I whispered.

To kill, to kill thoughtlessly, to kill for no purpose, to never use your prey, was a grave sin. One didn't kill *just* to kill. Animals had pure, good souls, and to kill and not use their bodies was to make a mockery of their souls, and possibly corrupt it and invite misfortune. I was already plagued by misfortune, I was sure, but I wouldn't make it worse and kill like this.

I put my bow on my back. "I – I'm sorry," I said to the not-Zaldi. "I thought you were . . . I'll make this right."

The not-Zaldi, or maybe just the weird-horse, would normally be a beautiful looking specimen, with a bay brown coat that seemed almost like it was forever touched with golden sunlight. I'd never seen another horse like it. Not that I'd seen that many horses in my life.

The weird-horse didn't seem to be paying much attention to me anymore, the most movement being in the ears, with one pointed in my direction and the other flicking about. I stepped towards it cautiously. If I could just yank out the arrow . . .

Hooves clattered and the weird-horse skittered away. For a brief second, I thought teeth snapped. I flinched back. "I'm trying to help!" I complained.

The weird-horse didn't seem interested in my reasons. I watched as it tried to step away, but its balance wobbled and it picked its hind hoof high. My hands dropped to my sides.

It couldn't walk. A horse that couldn't walk, couldn't run, was nothing but prey, even if it was a weird-horse. If it died, it'd be my fault. I couldn't walk away now, to let the weird-horse meet its unnatural fate and risk being haunted by the soul of a not-Zaldi. If the guilt didn't eat me up first. If I could just get the arrow *out*.

"Alright," I said. "Just . . . stay there for a minute, I guess."

I climbed up the rocks boxing the horse in, scrambling up to the top and scanning the horizon. The grasslands stretched on in one direction, the forest still a green smudge to the northeast, but to the west where the ground twisted and rolled and was sparse, I could see a lush cut where a creek ran. I couldn't see the rest of the weird-horse herd.

I glanced down at the weird-horse, but it didn't seem inclined to move. I called down, "I think your friends are gone. Don't go anywhere, and I'll be back."

It didn't take long to get over to the creek. I topped up my waterskin with as much as it could hold, then headed back to the weird-horse, keeping an eye out for flat stones or wide pieces of bark. I found a few and carried them back.

The weird-horse watched me dully as I used the stones I'd found and the natural curves of the rocks to create a little pool. I poured half of my waterskin in. I stepped back from it. "Here. Water," I said.

For several minutes, I thought maybe the weird-horse didn't want to drink, or didn't understand, or was simply ready to die and haunt me. Then it took laborious step after laborious step, leg jerking up in pain, towards the slowly trickling-away pool. It drank.

In the moment it drank, I lunged forward and snatched at the arrow. The angle was bad, and the flesh tore more than a little, but then it was in my hand and the horse was screaming and a hoof cracked against my leg.

I scrambled away on my hands, but the arrow was out. Now, the wound could heal cleanly.

The weird horse gave a decisive snort and went back to drinking and I rubbed at my thigh. The skin was already darkening with a bruise. "I just *helped* you," I grumbled.

The weird-horse finished drinking and limped away, water droplets falling from its mouth. At least there was no more foam around its lips. Blood no longer seemed to be oozing out from the wound, its path growing dark and crusty on its fur.

I sat back, studying it. The weird-horse took a few more experimental steps, but it still couldn't walk properly. I gave a great sigh. "You're definitely going to haunt me if you die." I rubbed my fingers over the ends of my hair. "I don't know where your friends are. You're on your own now. I know how that feels. It's not so bad, you know. It's manageable."

The weird-horse paid me little mind and lipped at the ground. It gave a soft nicker. "Oh, are you hungry? I guess I'm hungry too, now that I think about it. Do you eat like other horses, or is your diet more like the Zaldi after all?"

There was no response, which was probably a good thing.

I stood up. "Well, I guess I can get you something to eat for today. I'll make sure nothing comes along and kills you, at least. You'll probably be mostly better by tomorrow."

I went back to the grassland, used my knife to cut free an armful of long grasses, and carried it back to the weird-horse. It perked up a little after I set the grasses on the ground and backed away. It was a good sign it still had an appetite.

The two of us took our time finishing our meals. The weird-horse, a mess of snapping teeth and clomping hooves and flattened ears if I made even the slightest move towards it, made its limping way out of the rocks. It was painfully slow progress. I could take a casual stroll faster than it could walk.

Still, it wasn't like I could stop it.

"I guess one good thing came of this," I said to it, "now I know your kind aren't Zaldi. Or – maybe you're half Zaldi. Is that it? Was one of your parents a wild horse, and one a Zaldi?" The weird-horse, again, didn't speak back. The closest I got to a reply was it exhaling noisily.

I decided that, until I got evidence otherwise, this had to be a half Zaldi. It simply looked too odd to be *just* an ordinary horse, but it also clearly didn't have much in the way of demonic powers. If it did, then it would've given me worse than one bruise by now.

The half Zaldi took a meandering, limping path and I trailed after it. Before I knew it, the rest of the day had whiled away, and while the horse didn't lie down, I saw its eyes close, and I curled up under a shrub.

I awoke to the glow of the sun hitting my eyes, my shoulders and neck feeling sore and awkward. I rolled them to try and work them loose and cast a look around. The half Zaldi was gone.

I jumped to my feet, a mixture of anxious and relieved pumping through me. If it was gone, that had to mean it was recovered.

I spotted it just on the other side of a hill, munching at the grass and stumbling along. I could see from here that its leg still wasn't right. I grumbled and strode after it.

I got quite close before it noticed me, whipping its head around and snapping its teeth. With its ears flat back like that, it really did look snake-like. I wondered if the Zaldi maybe had different forms in the world of demons, and if that form was of a snake. People talked about the world of demons being a terrifying place, so perhaps demons tried to take on more familiar forms in our world, to better hide and wreak havoc.

I really didn't know much about demons, and it had been many generations since the Zaldi had last been seen, so a lot had been forgotten. Trying to remember things was like hearing the voice of birramona, as everyone called her, without being able to make out her words. I didn't think she was anyone's actual great-grandmother, but she'd been as kind and knowledgeable as one.

So many clan memories had been lost along with her. Along with everyone.

The crushing feeling was back, making me gasp, and I shoved it down again to focus on the half Zaldi in front of me. It snuffled through the grass calmly enough, as long as I didn't move. My stomach grumbled.

Deciding to ignore the gnashing teeth and such, I scoured a bare spot on the ground and conjured up a small fire, feeding it bits of grass. A thin bit of dark smoke rose into the sky, and for a moment, it was like it filled my nose and throat and I couldn't breathe. Then the half Zaldi made an angry sound, jarring me back to the present.

I carefully heated up the water in my waterskin, just enough to make it lukewarm, and then poured it into a curved rock I'd found, that kind of worked like a bowl. I added some of the grains I'd gathered, letting them soften and warm.

It was rather soupy and bland, but it was warmer than something foraged, and the cinders radiated heat to my toes, so I was satisfied.

The half Zaldi had wandered away again by the time I'd finished eating and buried the fire. There didn't seem to be any predators around, but there was a lone carrion bird winging circles around the sky, which I didn't think was a good sign.

Once, as a child, I'd seen a carrion bird eat an injured rabbit, even though the rabbit had still been alive at the start of it. For a carrion bird, all that mattered was blood.

The half Zaldi was much larger than a rabbit, but I still didn't like its chances. I could hardly leave it alone now.

I packed everything up and walked after the half Zaldi. It snapped at me some more with its serpentine head.

After that, things started to get blurry again.

The days were all alike, with the half Zaldi wandering about at a shamble, with me trailing in its wake. In a strange way, it was almost relaxing. At least, as long as ghosts didn't whisper on the wind after nightfall, nearly stopping my heart. With each passing day, the half Zaldi let me get a little bit closer. Sometimes I fetched water for both of us, or got it grass when it went onto rocky areas.

It was just me and the half Zaldi, and the rest of the world seemed to drop away.

One afternoon, I was munching on a roasted rabbit, and the half Zaldi folded its front legs and dropped onto its side. It lowered its head to the ground. In alarm, I raced over. It had been fairly energetic, and eating and drinking – it couldn't be dying. It just couldn't!

Its ears went back, and it flicked it's tail so the hairs stung my cheek, but I didn't care. It wasn't biting or kicking, and that was good enough for me. I felt along its wound. Its flesh was hot, but the fur was fine and soft. Its leg twitched a little, but it wasn't a violent movement.

The wound didn't seem swollen, nor was it oozing cursed puss, but it wasn't clean, either. I trickled a little bit of water over it, and used my fingers to gently get rid of dried blood and mud and bits of grass and seed that had stuck to it.

There was a dark scab over where the arrow had been. On the whole, I judged the half Zaldi was healing. I moved a few paces away and sat down, meeting its eye. "I guess you're just tired," I said to it. "You never lie down. You take a good nap now. I'll keep an eye out."

There was no real glimmer of understanding, but after a few minutes, its eyelids drooped shut.

I looked up at the sky. Listened to the wind as it whispered, and the clouds spoke messages.

"I know," I said into the sky. "I will avenge all of you. But I don't think this is a Zaldi. I think it's a clue. I'm the reason it's injured and alone. I can offer it the kindness I can't receive, at least for a while."

The voices in the air continued to whisper, but I thought they were a little gentler. The clouds dissolved into curls of white and then nothing but blue sky.

After some hours, the half Zaldi woke up and rocked to its feet in a wild movement. It studied me with one eye, ears flicking back and over, back and over, and then it snorted and tore up some grass.

I rested elbow on knee, hand on chin, and watched it. "Was that 'thank you' or 'you're still here'?" I asked.

The half Zaldi didn't answer me, but I did feel like I was a little closer to finding its thoughts.

As more days slipped past, the half Zaldi's leg seemed to get better. I saw it putting weight on it more often, and sometimes it did experimental little hops. I expected it to run far away from me at any time, but it didn't. It let me get quite close.

Once, I was bringing it some more grasses, and it walked right up and started munching on them out of my hands. I was too stunned to move, and the half Zaldi's ears were still flicked back, which I had figured out meant it was unhappy, but it still ate.

Then, it let me touch its neck. Its eye remained fixed on me, as I did so, so I just gently stroked it, until it had decided it'd had enough.

It was strange. I was used to dogs, and our herds of aurochs and mouflon, but the half Zaldi wasn't like any of them, but neither did it seem quite as wild as I'd always thought horses were. It was a strange being.

I was able to check the arrow wound a second time. It seemed to be almost entirely healed over, and the half Zaldi walked normal regularly, as long as the ground was relatively even. It watched me with angry eyes and flat ears, but it didn't run away or kick.

"You're feeling a lot better, aren't you?" I said to it one day, combing my fingers through its mane. "Pity we can't find your friends. The only horse tracks I can find are yours."

The half Zaldi snorted, and lipped at my side. Disappointed to not find food, it went back to sniffing at the ground. I almost smiled, watching it.

This close to it, I had a new appreciation for the size of the half Zaldi. Wild horses, at best, came up to my lower chest. The half Zaldi was closer in size to an auroch, it's shoulders around the same height as my own. Its frame was much different from an auroch, though, back being curved instead of having a straight spine.

It'd been a common pastime, as children, for us to try and ride the aurochs. We'd all taken turns scrambling up on backs and goading the auroch to walk around. It'd been fun, a soft memory of childhood I couldn't get back; but succeeding hadn't been comfortable.

Sitting on an auroch hurt. Less, if they were plump, but it was still a little like straddling a stick. I'd never been able to adjust my seat comfortably.

Looking at the half Zaldi, I thought – sitting on its back might not be so bad. I could picture a way to sit that might not be so awkward.

I glanced at its head, where it was still ripping up grass. It didn't mind me standing here and touching it at all. It was almost like it'd forgotten about me.

Before I could rethink my choice, I wound my hand into a fistful of mane and pushed off the ground, swinging one leg up.

I landed on its back with no problem. It jerked beneath me, pitching me forward onto the neck. The ground vanished and I stared at the sky and the half Zaldi screamed and gravity slid me down its back to thump on the ground.

My head banged into dirt and I saw hooves flash just above my eyes.

I didn't move as the half Zaldi stamped and snorted. Only when it quieted did I risk sitting up. It was staring at me angrily.

"Okay," I said, "you don't like that. I think I was right, though. You would be more comfortable than an auroch."

The half Zaldi snorted at that, gave a violent flick of its tail, and put its butt to me.

But it didn't go anywhere.

Chapter 3
Bound by Tooth and Claw

WITH THE HALF ZALDI much recovered, I focused more effort on finding food for myself, and on finding tracks that could lead me to a full Zaldi. I kept the creature in sight, and the half Zaldi seemed to do the same, because although we wandered around separately, neither of us lost track of the other.

On cold nights, I almost wished the half Zaldi was friendlier, because sleeping against it would, I imagined, be nice. It didn't seem interested in lying down and cuddling, though. It didn't seem interested in much, aside from food.

A couple of times I woke up in the blue and gold of dawn to the half Zaldi nudging me with its nose. I'd give it a pat, it'd grow disappointed tasting my clothes, and it would walk off.

It was walking well, now. Sometimes, when I believed it thought I wasn't looking, it would trot and canter, and it looked to be moving normally. I was glad. If it could just find its friends, it could go back to a normal life.

It still had friends to find.

I tried one other time, to ride the half Zaldi, but the result was the same. It would buck and rear and twist until I hit the ground. It seemed horses, ordinary or supernatural, were not inclined to allow people on their backs.

It was a pity. I thought the idea had merit. Horses were fast and strong. If they would work with humans, we could probably find lots of uses for them. Aurochs weren't good for much aside from meat and skin, and occasionally to carry heavy packs when we searched for a new summer campsite in the cold months.

I couldn't find any full Zaldi tracks, or even wild horse tracks, so I vaguely decided I needed a new approach. After all the days that'd passed as the world had turned gradually greener, I wasn't sure how far I was from where my clan had settled, or even what direction it was in.

Zaldi, I thought, didn't go that far from the lakes and rivers they lived in. If I strayed too much, then any Zaldi I did find wouldn't be one of the ones responsible for dragging off my people.

I'd still kill them, and free whatever poor souls they had snatched; but I wanted to save my people, not a faceless person from generations back. If I couldn't free someone, *anyone*, soon – the thought made me feel like I was the one eternally drowning, not them.

I needed height, if I was going to get the lay of the land, and landmarks, and the only landmarks were rivers or the forest that kept moving around on the horizon. Rivers always ran in low spots, and they twisted and turned and branched, and I didn't much like the idea of blindly following its curves.

At least, not while I was hunting Zaldi.

I chose to make for the forest. I remembered the direction it was in from the marsh, so all I had to do was get there and reverse it, to get a heading for the marsh. Also, forests had a lot more game to hunt than grasslands, and a lot more edible plants, too. It'd be a good chance to stock up.

I'd been collecting as I passed stuff, but still my supplies were dwindling. If I wasn't careful, I'd run out of food and be lost and starve to death before I could avenge my clan and free their souls.

I walked with purpose towards the forest, the smudge growing with every hour. I didn't look back, not really, but I could hear the faint clomp of hooves behind me. If the half Zaldi wanted to follow, it could follow. I wouldn't stop it.

Besides, it made me feel a little less alone.

It was a stupid feeling. The animal wasn't even entirely of this world. It probably didn't care about me at all.

I camped one night, in the shadow of a wind-bent tree. It was a proud, lonesome thing. I liked it. My little fire felt like a tiny beacon against the darkness of everything.

Come morning, I thought the half Zaldi had moved elsewhere without me before spotting it lying down. I didn't think it was asleep, from the way its ears twitched.

I gave it a solemn nod, ate some berries, and went back on my way.

The forest grew in size and scale before my very eyes. It looked dark and foreboding, with trees of oak and aspen spreading rich canopies. There were constant dots of movement to draw the eye, though whether from wind or animals, I couldn't yet tell.

Shrubs were growing thickly in the forest's shadow. The trunks out here were new and slender, but they gave me a slight chill. Forests, normally, were not a place to ever go alone. It felt odd to put my back to it as I knelt down to strip some plants of their edibles.

I wonder how far away the portal to the dead was hidden. Hopefully deep in the heart, along with its guardian wolves.

A rustling, not quite a breeze, made me look up. Standing in the shadows, was a white stag.

My body ran hot and cold. A white stag. The stag of my people. I stepped towards it.

Ears went up and it bolted north. "No – wait!" I cried. Surely it had something to tell me, something to show me. Surely it was a message from my family – I need only catch it, follow it –

Something echoed in the distance.

I froze, nearly in the forest proper, looking up. The half Zaldi's ears were pricked.

The echo repeated, a ringing wolf's howl.

My blood ran cold.

I was running before I could process it. Wolves – wolves would circle and kill me, or maybe worse if I accidentally ran into a portal to the world of the dead. If they were still in the woods – if I could make it back to that lone tree and climb it – maybe – maybe –

The half Zaldi was gone, a figure rapidly dwindling to a speck as I ran. I ran, feet pounding the ground, breath sharp in my lungs. Howls rang behind me. A rough bark filled the air.

Move it legs, move it!

The half Zaldi was twisting as it ran – was its leg not healed? Was it –

Why . . . why was it coming *back*?

I didn't have the breath to shout at it as it charged up and circled around me. It gave a loud call. I looked back at the wolf pack, snarling and barking. Their legs ate up the ground.

Hard pain on my arm made me stumble. My eyes snapped to the half Zaldi. It kept pace with me. Nipped my arm again. Tossed its head up and down.

Oh, I realized, and twined my arms in its mane and threw myself up just as teeth snapped at my heels.

It was like being released from a bow. The half Zaldi surged beneath me and the world dropped away, the howls of the wolves fading. I clung on tightly, eyes shut, wind whistling by my ears. I couldn't catch my breath. I was going to throw up.

We kept running, and running. I didn't throw up. How far away from the forest were we now? Cautiously I lifted my head and cracked open my eyes.

The world was flying by, faster than a bird could wing. The ground was a blur of colour and plants appeared and vanished in the blink of an eye. The wind stung my face and whistled in my ears, and the rhythm of the half Zaldi pounded through me.

I'd never felt so alive.

A laugh bubbled out of me, a strange, shrieking thing torn away by the wind in the instance it was born. Every part of me tingled.

We ran and ran, and then, with the forest far behind us, almost invisible, the half Zaldi slowed. It moved through a rolling canter and a bouncy trot, and then came to a stop.

My heart pounded and my chest heaved, and I felt like everything had to be reoriented.

A hard nip on my shin, an irritated breath and a stamp. I blinked hard. "Oh, right." I slid off the half Zaldi's back, and my legs promptly gave out from under me.

I made a shaky sound and doubled over, my whole body trembling. The half Zaldi shoved its nose in my face, snuffling. I raised an unsteady hand and rubbed its face. "Thank you. I'd be dead if not for you."

It shoved its nose against me again, then gave a contented sound and began lipping at the grass. My stomach gave a grumbling noise. "I think you have the right idea."

I settled back against a rock and ate some seeds and a little piece of roasted meat. The half Zaldi pawed at the ground, lips still snuffling the grass.

"You know," I said, "when you do things like that, you seem less supernatural and more ordinary. But you're definitely not an ordinary animal. You're much more intelligent than I thought. Certainly more than a mouflon. Maybe more than an auroch. Maybe even as smart as a dog."

It flicked its tail in response. I continued on, "We're going to stick together. Look out for each other. I know you can't speak, but I can, and you clearly can hear me, so I need something to call you by. I'm sure you have your own name, but since I can't learn it, I'll have to give you one. Let's see . . ." I thought about it for a minute. "I think I'm going to call you Behorra. You're a girl, after all."

The reaction I got was a snort and a twitch of the ears, which I thought was a sort of acceptance. I stretched my legs out. "So, uh, where exactly have you taken us?"

Around us was nothing but grasses and shrubs and copses of young trees. I could hear the faint trickle of a stream. All I knew was the forest was some distance east.

Behorra kept chomping on grass until she found the stream and nosily took a drink. I rolled to my feet and went to refill my waterskin.

The wind picked up and hissed in my ear, and the clouds in the sky above curled ominously. A threatening shadow briefly took shape in the water. "Don't worry," I said to everyone. "I haven't forgotten."

I decided I, or rather, we, as I'd now have to think of things, would follow the little run of water downstream. I didn't really have a better idea of how to orient myself – the woods were out of the question, after all. At least the stream was likely to meet up with a larger river, and there were always more opportunities along a river.

I hoped, perhaps foolishly, that my ancestors would send the stag again. The next time, I wouldn't quite so blindly follow it and anger more uncanny beings.

As we walked, I decided to set some rules with Behorra. I was fine to let her do what she wanted most of the time, but there were definitely going to be instances like the wolves again. I had to make sure she could understand what I was thinking.

She didn't have much interest in learning. At first, she didn't even like me whistling. Whistles were just the best option I could think of, to tell her things like 'go' or 'come'. After all, they were what we used with dogs.

Behorra certainly wasn't as eager to please as a dog, but I also didn't think she was as obstinate as aurochs were. You couldn't get them to do anything unless you were dragging them by the face and smacking them on the butt.

"It's for emergencies," I told her. "We don't know what's going to happen."

Still, she didn't like the whistles. I could only hope she really was learning.

The stream became a creek, and the creek became a river. The plants grew lush and green, and everything rustled with game. I saw small animals and birds hourly. With the steady amount of prey, I was able to eat quite well. Behorra decided that maybe fires weren't so terrifying after all.

The river's course turned twisted and rough, full of rocks and churning water, until it dropped sharply and spread into a lake.

It wasn't a very big lake. The other side was quite near, to the point where I thought I could easily swim the distance. I didn't try, though. I didn't think Behorra would know how to get me out if I grew tired. She wasn't a full Zaldi, after all.

I waded through the shallows, scattering little fish. I wondered if my presence would tempt a Zaldi, or another demon, up to the surface. Or perhaps they would be drawn to Behorra.

On the shore, Behorra suddenly pricked her ears, gave a nicker, and trotted ahead. I hurried out onto dry land and chased after her.

Soon I saw what she had. Out in the lake, horses were playing.

They were normal wild horses, their furry heads and thick manes dark with water. I stopped and watched as they waded through the shallows to the deeper reaches. Out in the lake they were swimming, heads bobbing just above the surface and nostrils flaring.

"I don't think those are your friends," I said to Behorra, who was watching the horses play with interest.

That fact didn't seem to matter to her. She whinnied loudly and trotted out into the lake. One of the wild horses called back to her. I found a good stump to sit against and settled down.

Water splashed and soon Behorra was drenched. The horses communicated for a brief while in the shallows, the water making it hard to see. Behorra waded out into the deeper water.

She playfully batted her nose at one of the swimming horses.

She wasn't swimming.

The other horses around her were definitely swimming. I could tell by how low to the surface their rocking heads were. But Behorra – I could still see the top of her neck, her withers, her rump. She wasn't swimming. She was just standing. She moved through the lake almost effortlessly, her hooves able to reach the bottom.

Oh.

The realization was world-shifting. Behorra and the other horses played happily, oblivious. "I was wrong," I whispered.

"You're not a Zaldi at all. None of you are. Just a different horse . . . no wonder we think you demons, if you can walk where some horses must swim."

It changed everything and nothing all at once. Behorra was just a horse. A wonderful, intelligent horse. And I had no idea how to identify a real Zaldi, or how to find one.

I hadn't wanted her to be a demon, I realized, even partially. The crushing feeling returned a little, as after all this time, I was still so, so achingly far from avenging my clan.

No wonder their ghosts seemed so dissatisfied. No wonder the stag had tried to lead me away. They must think themselves doomed to an eternity of trying to flee the world of demons, only to always be dragged back. I whispered a prayer to soothe them.

I had not forgotten. I would free their souls.

I just was no longer sure how.

Behorra chose to stay with me, instead of the wild horses, and I chose to leave the small lake behind. I found a river draining from the lake and chose to follow it. Around us, the scrub land was beyond the early shoots of spring and well on its way to the glory of summer. It would be a while until it reached its fruitful peak.

It was a strange sort of life I seemed to now have. Summers were normally peaceful times, where we looked after the herds and watched as the edible plants we sowed grew and items were repaired and, sometimes, other clans were met and traded with. It was a busy *people* time.

Instead, this was going to be a summer of me and a horse and no one else. It was odd, but still, it was me *and*, and that was okay with me.

I succeeded, once, in convincing Behorra to let me ride her again. I didn't blame her for not enjoying someone sitting on her back, but if we ever needed to flee in a hurry, I wanted to have some say in where we went.

Behorra was smart, but she wasn't that smart.

It took me a while to figure out the best way to sit, and I found that wrapping my legs around her belly kept me the most secure. We practiced a bit, and eventually worked out a system where if I nudged her with my heels, she'd go forward, and if I pressed one leg against her side, she'd turn. Stopping was trickier, but if I sat up like I was going lean backwards she would eventually slow.

After that she got sick of the riding and started nipping at my leg. It didn't hurt much when she bit me, but it still wasn't nice.

We kept following the river and came across a marshy spot. Behorra wandered away from the shore, to where the grasses were drier. I let her go and carefully picked my way along the marshy area. There were some good greens to cut or dig up with fish swimming between stalks, and despite my lack of spear, I made a few catches to eat for dinner.

The bugs were getting bad, this far into the season, so I didn't linger by the river. I went to go catch up to Behorra.

I came around a couple of trees and froze. Behorra was not alone.

If she'd met up with some wild horses, or even a herd of deer, I wouldn't have been overly surprised. But it wasn't an animal I was seeing. It was people.

They were four men of varying ages, and they crept in crouches towards Behorra. For a minute, I thought they believed her a Zaldi and were hoping to sneak by.

Then I saw their bows.

Hunters.

CHAPTER 4
MEMORIES OF BEING HUMAN

BEHORRA PAID THE HUNTERS little attention, likely viewing other humans the way I viewed the wild herds. Rocks skidded underneath my feet as I ran.

One of the hunters stood up and drew his bow.

I gave a piercing whistle and crashed into his side. I didn't know where the arrow went. Behorra whinnied and took off. I rolled in the dirt and sprang to my feet. A hand curled around my clothes and jerked me. Someone was cursing.

I twisted, scratching at the hand and kicking one of the men in his lower region. A searing line of heat ran across my upper arm. I punched one's nose. A shout in my ear.

I bit something, but then hands were off me and I stumbled away and I took off running.

The men shouted. An arrow flew over my head. I ran, following Behorra's tracks, and kept running. It wasn't until the hunters were small shapes behind me that I whistled again.

After the third whistle, I could see her up ahead. She'd stopped running and was looking in my direction, ears pricked.

When she saw me, she began to trot over. I slowed to a walk. My arm burned, and I could feel blood running down it. Behorra sniffed at me, sneezing when she took a breath full of the scent of my blood.

I stroked her face. "And *this* is why I'm trying to teach you signals. Do you get it now?"

She didn't make any sign of acknowledgment or agreement, she just continued to nudge me with her nose. "Okay, okay, stop." I pushed her nose away and inspected my arm.

It wasn't a deep wound, just a cut line across the width of my upper arm. A small blade point protruded from it. I yanked it out and tossed it to the ground, and the blood dripped from the wound thickly. Just moving my left arm made it hurt.

I sighed and pressed my hand over it, scanning the ground. The pressure gave it a welcome burn. Behorra followed me closely as I wandered about, searching for a plant with wide, flat leaves. Eventually I managed to find ones that were passable and layered them on over the cut.

I used the little bit of spare cord I had to keep it on. It was awkward and messy and unpleasant to tie, holding one end in my teeth and having only my right hand to make a knot with. It was a lopsided knot, but it kept the leaves on.

My heart ached with longing for my mother and sister, both of whom had deft and clever fingers that had patched up many injuries over my life. If they were here, they'd tell me exactly what I was doing wrong and fix me up and my arm wouldn't hurt nearly as much.

Behorra stuck her nose in my face, and abruptly I realized how close to watering my eyes were. I took a couple deep breaths and spread the almost-tears over my face. "I'm fine," I told her. "Probably hurts less than yours did." I stood up. "Come on, let's find some water."

The two of us struck off in a direction, going at an easy pace. I kept glancing back over my shoulder, thinking I'd see hunters chasing us down, but I never saw a soul.

I found a small pond, and the two of us settled down to rest.

The next morning I slept to well past sunrise, and was roused mostly by an angry throbbing in my arm. My joints felt thick and stiff from my elbow to my fingers. It sent stings of pain whenever I moved it.

I felt around where I'd tied the leaves, and my arm didn't seem particularly swollen, so I figured I was okay. I submerged my hand in the cool water of the pond for a minute, which made it feel a little better. Behorra took a long drink next to me, and I decided we should continue on.

It wasn't long before a series of offshoots from the pond spread and widened and turned the area into a mucky marsh. It pulled at my feet. I pushed Behorra over to the edge where the ground was firmer.

The marsh was noisy with bugs and birds and frogs. They called and sang and splashed and filled the air. I enjoyed listening to all the sounds of life.

There were so many sounds, I didn't think twice about them until Behorra, who was walking ahead, abruptly stopped and snorted, prancing on the spot.

"What's wrong?" I asked. "What –"

I stopped, staring down at the hunter standing chest deep in the mud. It looked like he'd been struggling and stuck there for quite some time. He stared up at Behorra, then looked at me.

He was younger than I'd originally thought, being around the same age as me. The bead strands braided into his dark hair still had clean colours and good edges, so it couldn't have been more than a few years since he came of age. His eyes were dark and soft, and the thick eyebrows were raised quizzically. He had a splattering of mud on his cheeks.

"Hello," he said.

I stared at him, then looked around anxiously for the other hunters in his party.

"They're not here," he said. "They went back to get some more men."

I glanced up and down what little I could see of him. "Are you stuck?"

"Annoyingly."

I gave a small nod, then walked past him on the shore.

"What, you're just leaving like that?"

I glanced back at him. "You tried to hunt Behorra."

"Be – it's a horse! Horses are food! You can't blame me for that. It wasn't even my idea."

I shrugged. "And it's not my fault you're stuck."

"The ground *looked* solid, okay?" It sounded like he'd tried to convince people of that already.

"Uh-huh." I crouched down and studied him. "How long have you been stuck in there?"

". . . I'd rather not say."

I looked at the ground. "Your friends left a couple hours ago, at least."

"So you can track, then."

I studied the young man some more. On closer inspection, his skin looked a little pale, and the colour faded, like skins left too long in the sun, or a child out too long in the cold. "You can't hunt Behorra when out," I said.

"Don't touch the horse. Got it. Figured that out after yesterday. Though I'm guessing you'll be long gone by the time I'm pulled out."

I rolled my eyes. Maybe, I thought, he wasn't always the brightest.

I stood up and wrapped my hand around Behorra's head to pull her close to the marsh's edge. On the ground were a few things the other hunters had left behind, including a long length of cording. I pushed Behorra into position, which made her stamp her feet and toss her head.

The young man watched me quietly as I fiddled with the rope. It took me a couple tries, but I found that if I tied a loop around her belly, and then used another length to connect it over her chest, it was reasonably secure. I had to keep stopping her from nibbling it.

I used the longest length of rope and attached one end to Behorra and tossed the other to the young man. He wrapped it around his hands. "Ready?" He nodded. I clicked my tongue at Behorra and encouraged her forward.

She balked and danced a little at the heavy resistance, but after a minute she calmed and grew used to it and walked forward steadily, if slowly. The mud made great squelching and sucking sounds as, bit by bit, it loosened its grip on the young man and he moved closer to shore.

It took several long minutes, but then he was almost at the shore and I was able to help drag him out. He was coated in mud, and shivering, but free.

"Thank you," he said, as I undid the ropes I'd tied around Behorra. She picked her feet up high and danced around once free of them.

I gave the young man a shrug. I could feel him watching me.

"What's wrong with your arm?" he asked.

"Nothing."

"Yes there is." He stood up suddenly, spooking Behorra. He grabbed my left arm and pulled it towards him before I could react. I hissed.

"What kind of binding is this? It's terrible!" he exclaimed.

"I did what I could!" I jerked my arm free.

"That doesn't make it *good*. Here, let me –" I stepped back from him and his hands, my nerves on edge. He gave me a look. "You're just asking for it to get worse, you know. The least I can do is tie on something properly for you. You did pull me out, after all."

I didn't say anything for a minute. He was still shivering a little, and he swayed a tad on his feet. He probably hadn't eaten all day, either. Even if he wanted to try something, which seemed unlikely, he was in no state to be a threat.

"Do what you want," I said.

The sunny smile was at odds with the pale complexion. He gestured for me to sit down somewhere, and started rummaging through his gear. Surprisingly little mud had gotten inside. I glanced at Behorra, who was watching me with twitching ears.

I found a good dry spot and sat down, legs crossed. The young man sat down next to me and I let him undo the wrapping on my arm. The knot came undone embarrassingly easily.

Behorra came closer, then backed up, snorting and tossing her head. She did that a couple times, then danced around to the other side of me.

"What's she doing?" the young man asked, as he opened a pouch.

"She doesn't like you," I said.

He pulled a face at that. From the pouch he drew what looked like a mushy cube of herbs. It had a strong smell that made me wrinkle my nose. "What *is* that?"

"Some healing herbs my clan traded for. You put them on a wound under the wrappings, and it keeps evil out," he said.

"Oh."

Behorra tossed her head and flared her nostrils as the young man smeared some of the herb mush on my arm. It felt cool. He tied a strip of scraped-thin hide over top. "There," he said, "all done."

I stood up and backed away from him, rolling my arm in a circle. Behorra nudged at me nervously, and clearly didn't like the smell. She sneezed. The young man continued to watch me, the look in his eyes strange. "That horse . . . I've never seen one act like it."

"Okay." I picked up my things.

He stood up. "Where are you going?"

"On my way. Your people are coming for you. You'll be fine to wait here."

"That's not – are you out here alone? Did you get lost? You could come back with us, we could get you home –"

"I am not lost. I am fine."

"Are you sure? What clan are you from? I didn't think any other clan had out camps in this area."

"I see no reason to tell you." I gave Behorra a quick whistle and started walking along the shore.

"Can I at least get your name?" he asked.

"No," I said over my shoulder.

"Please?"

I kept walking, picking up the pace to leave him behind.

"Won't you –" I hopped down over a few stones, a little run off babbling away into the distance. "I'm one of the Oin Zuria!" he shouted. "I'm Kemen!"

I distractedly waved a hand to shut him up, but I didn't look back, and Behorra and I continued on our way.

For a few days the two of us wandered west and south, chasing game and looking for clues of Zaldi. I found plenty of food, but nothing else. I didn't see any more people, which was good. I didn't want to put Behorra in more danger, and I certainly didn't want to explain myself to anyone.

I knew moving around in the wild, alone, was dangerous. Deadly. It was a sure-fire way to get myself killed.

But someone from another clan wouldn't understand. I was the last of the Bizkor Oiloa. The souls of all my people rested on me. I had to set them free.

At some point, I started to think that maybe I'd been traveling so much that my mind was getting confused, because things began to look familiar. Had I somehow gotten turned around? Was I just retracing my steps?

A chill began to settle on me, one that went through to my heart and bones.

I knew this landscape. I recognized the rolls of the land, the curve of the river in the distance, that tree with – yes, a broken arrow in one of its upper branches. I'd, somehow, managed to find my way back to the area my clan had settled in for the summer.

Things swirled inside me, and the crushing feeling was back, threatening to squeeze me out of existence. I had to stop and bend over and force myself to breathe. Behorra sniffed my hair, but otherwise seemed at ease.

"Okay," I said to myself. "You can do this. Besides, you need to find clues to the Zaldi. You can do this."

I straightened and bravely forged ahead.

Thoughts pushed at me as I drew closer and I pushed them back. I had to focus. Focus.

I stopped when I could see the settlement.

It was worse than when I'd left it. I knew it would be, but it still made something in me tear. More homes had collapsed, and plants were growing tall and thick through every space they could. The clan idol was the tallest thing, now standing at a tilt.

It was a desolate place, where the wilds were overtaking the pitiful stake of humanity.

I scrubbed at my face repeatedly as I walked down the slope towards it. My hand drifted to my father's atlatl, fingers running over its familiar form.

I told myself that this wasn't home anymore, that I needed to keep myself grounded in reality, lest I find myself walking amongst the ghosts of my ancestors. Still, something in me twisted and cracked and I could hardly breathe or walk.

There really was no one here.

Much of the damage of that day had been obscured, scoured away by nature. The tracks were practically gone, and I wasn't sure what else I could find.

I sifted through a few of the homes, just in case there was . . . something. I didn't know what I was looking for, or what I wanted to find. I just wanted something.

I found nothing of the Zaldi. Just the pieces of our lives, from homes to clothes to baskets to arrows . . .

Arrows.

I stopped and picked up an arrow lying in the grass. There was nothing odd about finding an arrow on the ground – we dropped ones all the time, or misplaced them with bad shots – but something about this arrow stuck out to me.

Oh.

It wasn't one of my clan's arrows.

We tied the arrowhead on by crossing, not wrapping, and the fletching of this one spiraled in the opposite direction. It was an arrow made and used by someone not from my clan.

Someone, or some*thing*.

Humans didn't attack other humans, generally speaking. Sure, people fought, and sometimes those fights got physical, and on occasion someone wound up dead. But no one set out with the intent of killing another person. At least, no one alive did.

Other creatures, on the other hand . . .

That wasn't to say that this arrow couldn't have come from a Zaldi; the tip had old blood, so if the Zaldi had been shot in the past, it could have fallen out as it thundered through here. We told stories of ghastly hunts, of souls who chased prey even after death and had little care for what type of creature the prey was. This arrow could be from such a hunt, though it felt too solid, too real.

Or perhaps, someone else was also hunting down these Zaldi, and that's why there was an arrow here.

The Zaldi had taken my *entire* clan; it seemed likely this wasn't the first time they'd dragged off groups of people. The question was, where had this arrow come from? Our world, or the other?

I studied it. The arrowhead shape was undistinctive, but the stone had some dark veining in it. The fletching was from common birds – understandable, since that was replaced most often. The shaft, though, was from a wood where, one year, the tree had been dyed.

It wasn't a common practice, even less so in recent generations, as the art of it had dwindled to live in fewer and fewer clans. Certain trees had importance – ones that grew where our ancestors had done great things that restored the balance between our world and the world of demons. Some of our ancestors had chosen to mark those trees by dyeing tree rings. That way, no one would cut them down by mistake.

Such trees were few and far between. Why would someone make an arrow from such a tree? Had something happened? What required a sacred arrow?

A human had definitely shot it. Its touch was fatal to demons and spirits.

Right. First, start with the source.

There weren't many such trees to investigate. In fact, I was only reasonably confident I could find one. My father had told me about where one was. Far to the north, on the shore of a lake where the waters were clear and the bottom was sandy. If you followed the stars and passed the carved stones, you would reach it.

It wasn't an easy journey, but it was the only lead I had to figuring out what exactly had happened, and why, and how to avenge my people. Perhaps, if I was lucky, I'd find an ally in my quest.

I straightened up and tucked the odd arrow away with the others in my quiver. Behorra was happily ripping up the tall grasses. To her, this place was the same as any other. To me, it made pieces of myself break off.

Something was burning inside me. "Come on," I said thickly to Behorra. "Let's get out of here."

I walked north, and eventually Behorra followed. I felt like I had an itch on the back of my head, between my shoulder blades, and I forced myself to not look back. If I did, I wasn't sure what I'd do.

Behorra and I were forced to turn east for a little while by the waterways, but at night I'd track our position by the stars, and I was sure I could get us going in the right direction again. The constellations burned bright, both in the night sky and in my memory. Reading the stars was something that'd always come to me naturally.

As the days passed, I thought we were making fairly good progress. As much as I wanted to rush ahead, Behorra got tired if she ran for too long, and I had to be mindful of gathering food and water. Unlike a horse, I couldn't find something to eat anywhere on the ground.

Then I woke up one morning feeling like my lower gut was about to rip itself apart.

I'd gotten *cramps.*

CHAPTER 5
THE HUMAN BEGUILES THE STAG

MOST OF THE TIME, I was an excellent example of health. People once remarked how strong and fit and capable I was. But things had changed shortly after I came of age; most months passed fine, but some months I had horrible, gut-wrenching cramps.

It'd never posed a problem for me in the past. I'd spend a few days off my feet, and I'd eat a light and cold porridge my mother or sister would make, and then I'd be back to normal. As long as I wasn't moving around, the pain wasn't that bad.

But I wasn't with my clan now.

The first day or two was usually pretty manageable, and came and went in waves, so at least I got a warning. I'd have to find some place to rest for a few days, but the real problem was food. I'd already been eating small amounts; I didn't have enough to last me several days of not hunting and gathering.

First things first, I told myself. Find a safe place.

Behorra walked near me, constantly coming over to give me a sniff. Perhaps she noticed I wasn't moving as fast as I normally did. Perhaps she smelt blood.

I got lucky, for the ground was full of rocks and crevices, and large bushes were growing everywhere. I found a large stone where one side had been worn in and smoothed, with some shrubs growing next to it, which had caused the ground to soften a little. It offered only a little protection, but it would block a decent amount of wind, and it was more comfortable than sleeping on rocks.

I set most of my gear down, while Behorra tried some of the shrub's leaves. She decided she didn't like them.

"Right," I said. "I need to find food while I still can. You stay here and watch this, hm?" She started eating some grass.

I went out with the bare minimum to see what food I could scrounge up. There wasn't much to find, and to my dismay, the sun was swiftly crossing the sky and dipping towards the horizon.

I was about to resign myself to days of starving when I caught a whiff of smoke and blood on the breeze. I knew in my head I should keep away, but curiousity got the better of me, and I followed the smell.

Soon I could see a thin thread of smoke rising to the sky. I lowered myself and crept through the scrub, the source revealing itself in the increasing gloom.

It was an out camp. Four men were cutting up a couple deer carcasses and securing the lids on baskets bursting with foodstuffs. I could smell it all from here, and it made my mouth water. They had so *much* of it.

The idea in my head put a little wiggle of discomfort in me. I knew it was wrong, cruel, even, to take the fruits of others' labours. I shouldn't steal. But I had next to nothing, I wasn't going to be able to move much, if at all, for days, and they surely wouldn't miss *one* basket, would they?

The smell of fire and food kept me mesmerized until there was almost no sun, and the hunters were settling into one of the huts to rest.

You really shouldn't do this, whispered the rational part of my mind. The rest of me whispered, *food! Food!*

I snuck towards the out camp.

I kept my steps soft as I crept past the huts and the smoldering remains of the fire. They'd tied a large skin blanket over the pile and staked it to the ground, to deter animals, but that wasn't a challenge for me.

I yanked the stakes out and flipped the blanket back, feeling for a full basket of a size I could easily carry in my arms.

A noise behind me.

I froze, listening. It was probably just one of the hunters turning over in sleep. I pulled a basket towards me.

I was jerked back by my clothes, a voice hissing, *"Thief."*

I rammed my hand back, felt my palm meet a nose. The grip on my clothes loosened enough for me to tear free. I twisted around, throwing a punch and missed. Something drove into my stomach, sending a spasm of pain through me.

I caught myself on the ground and tugged on his ankle. He hit the ground and I pressed my hands over his mouth to keep him from shouting. I had no idea how I was going to get out of this.

A stone was swung into my arm, hitting me right where I was cut. My arm buckled and I toppled to the side, a small moan escaping me. The hunter paused, then hauled me half off the ground. "Aren't you . . ."

Curious eyes reflected what little light there was. The hunter from the marsh.

"Why –" Someone else made a sleepy sound and gave a cracking stretch.

I was abruptly shoved away. "Get out of here, *now*," he hissed.

I didn't know why he was letting me go. I didn't think the other hunters were likely to be in agreement.

I pushed myself to my feet and ran.

Behorra was glad to see me back, but I didn't spend much time greeting her. I just threw myself down on the ground and fell asleep.

Come morning, my gut wasn't worse, exactly, but it definitely wasn't better, and I still needed to find more food. The sun was well risen before I managed to drag myself up and go look for something.

I found some bitter, unripened berries, and quashed them miserably between my teeth. I longed for something sweet and cool, but fruit trees were months away from being ready.

I sat down by the berry bush, wondering if there was something under the soil I could dig up. I hated eating bugs, but at this point I was desperate.

There was something under the bush.

Not something natural. A basket. I wrestled it out. A well-made basket, with a white footprint stamped on the lid. I pulled it open. It was full of shoots, dandelions, dead nettles, and even some willow bark. A few strips of dried meat had been added as well.

I didn't have to wonder who had left this, but I did wonder why. The hunter from the marsh was hardly even a passing acquaintance. I had tried to steal from him. Why would he go out of his way to hide food for me? It didn't benefit him in any way.

Still, food was food, and I wasn't in a position to turn it down. I picked up the basket and carried it back to the rest of my things.

Behorra tried to eat some of it, but I kept her out of it. She could eat just about anything growing on the ground. I was not so lucky.

The next few days were a blur in my mind. I spent hours dozing on and off, curled around my stomach while it attempted to rip itself apart. The most I moved was when I used tiny amounts of water to clean blood off myself and forced some food down. I kept wanting to throw up. Once I managed a fire to brew some willow tea, which made me feel a little better for a short time.

My head was pounding and felt heavy by the last day, but I felt less like I was going to die, and the blood had stopped coming. I got myself passably tidied up, at least for now, and worked on consolidating my supplies and gear. It all felt so heavy. I considered waiting another day before moving on.

I could hear pebbles and stones rolling, and grass rustling, and I called out to Behorra, "Finished eating?"

"What?" someone said.

I went still and slowly lifted my head, seeing it was far too late to do anything about the hunters who were approaching me.

The hunter from the marsh was struggling to smother an anxious look, but I focused on the other three. Two had bows, one had a set of spears, and all of them were older and well built.

I swallowed as they stared at me in astonishment. "Hello," I managed.

"What's a woman like you doing out here alone?" asked one of them, wrinkling his nose as he looked over my hidey-hole.

I pressed my lips shut.

"Wait, hold on, isn't that – it is!" One of them flashed a triumphant look. "I told you I thought we were missing a basket! She stole it!"

"I didn't," I said.

"Don't lie," one snapped. "That's our clan's basket *right there* and you are not one of our clan."

"You owe us for that food."

I rose slowly to my feet, trying not to sway slightly. My insides turned cold. I didn't have surprise on my side, and the one me, tired and weak as I was, against the four of them – I didn't like those odds.

"Got nothing else to say, little thief?"

I shifted my weight. One had a knife.

"You're gonna pay us ba –"

The hunter from the marsh rammed his knee between legs. "Run!" he shouted at me, yanking a skin over another's head.

I snatched up my things and bolted for it, stumbling. I gave a sharp whistle once, twice, then heard a whinny. Behorra trotted over and I scrambled up on her back, clinging tightly and digging my heels in. One of the men shouted and she took off.

Behorra ran at a steady canter, and I focused on just trying not to fall off or lose anything.

Why had he done that? Letting me go that night, leaving me food – that could be because I pulled him out of the marsh. But why would he fight his own clansmen? Why let me, who *had* intended to be a thief and got caught, go?

It didn't make any sense.

Well, it didn't matter in the end. I doubted I'd ever see him again.

The hunters had vanished behind us. Behorra slowed to a plodding walk and I slipped off her back, leaning on her shoulder for support. Her ears were back. "Sorry," I said, "My fault."

She snorted. Maybe she forgave me. It was hard to tell.

Quickly I grew too tired to keep walking and picked a spot beneath a tree to rest. It broke the wind and trapped what little heat of the sun there was, so it was good enough. Behorra had carried me quite a distance, so I risked a little fire for a couple hours.

I felt better after that, and cleaned up so I could move further on. I didn't want to take more risks than I had to until the hunters were far, far behind.

We walked a short way, with Behorra stopping and looking back frequently, ears pricked. I never saw anything. I wondered if, like dogs, horses could sometimes sense things that were not of this world.

I pushed onwards, stepping over the gnarled roots of a tree. Behorra looked back again and nickered. I sighed. "What are you – oh."

In the distance, coming over a hill, was a hunter. Specifically, the hunter from the marsh.

I frowned at his approaching figure.

Once he noticed me leaning against the tree, waiting, he picked up the pace. He was breathless as he approached. Behorra pranced around anxiously.

"What do you want?" I asked.

"I was worried about you."

I raised my eyebrows. "I'd be more worried about yourself. You stole from your people, attacked your own clansman – people will be furious. Those are the things that get someone exiled."

He avoided my gaze. "Well, yeah, no one's very happy with me at the moment, I'm sure." He gave a careless shrug. "It'll work out, though. I spend a few days 'lost' in the wilderness, and they'll be more worried than upset. By the time I head back, relief with overshadow whatever else they think of me."

"That's a very risky plan."

"I suppose. Not as risky as whatever you're doing, though. What you're doing out here . . ." His eyes roved over my gear. "I don't know what happened, but you should go back to your clan. They must be worried about you."

It was my turn to avoid looking at him, things twisting and tensing inside of me. "No one's worried about me."

"It's your *clan*, of course they are –"

"No, they aren't. They're dead."

59

"What? Everyone?"

"Yes. All of them. Except for me."

The blood drained from his face and his mouth worked. "All – why – *how* – the entire – that – that's . . ." He cleared his throat. "Can I ask, which . . . when . . .?"

"The Bizkor Oiloa. Now I am the last."

". . . I know – knew – of your clan. They met and traded with the Oin Zuria many times."

"I was never a part of that. And I don't care. Right now, all that matters is I avenge them."

He blinked. "Avenge? You mean – it wasn't fire or disease?"

"No." I focused on the curl of the clouds, trying to push out words thick in my throat. "I was out. Foraging. I came back, and . . . I thought it was the Zaldi. I thought the demon horses had dragged them all away."

"The Zaldi? – Oh." He looked at Behorra. "So I take it she's not a Zaldi."

"No. She's just a horse."

"Are you still hunting actual Zaldi?"

I shifted my weight. My throat burned. "I . . . had planned to. But . . . I am beginning to think some – something else was responsible."

"What?"

"I am not sure. The only clue I have found is a hunter's sacred arrow."

"A – a sacred arrow?! You mean this could've been done by hu –"

"I don't know!" I snapped. "I don't know."

He swallowed. "Whatever is going on, I don't think you should continue doing this. It could be anything, even . . ." He stepped towards me. "Please, let me, let us, help."

My mind felt as sluggish as a frozen river. "What?"

"I told you, the Oin Zuria know the Bizkor Oiloa. For this to have happened to your clan – come back with me. Tell people what happened. We will help you. We'll –"

"You'll do nothing!" I pushed myself away from the tree. "You won't speak a word of this! You may not be involved, but can you guarantee that *no one* in your clan had a part in this? Do you have the ability to know each and every one of their thoughts?"

". . . No."

"Then don't offer aid when I may find the opposite."

He shrank back.

I picked up my things and marched over to Behorra. She snuffled at my hands and licked one of my palms.

"W – wait," he said to my back. "Don't do this. You're a human. Humans aren't meant to do things alone."

I stroked Behorra's face. "I'm not alone. Not anymore."

I didn't let myself look back as Behorra and I walked away. I left the hunter from the marsh behind, the feel of the gaze on my back burning, and that crushing feeling making my chest tight and my breath thick.

Even if I knew everything, knew who to trust, I was the last one. That meant everything fell to me and me alone.

Chapter 6
A Story Lives in Firelight

A REASONABLE PERSON WOULD'VE turned around and gone home. It turned out the hunter from the marsh was not a reasonable person.

At first, I did think he was being reasonable and had left me alone. Then, Behorra kept stopping and looking back again, and when I turned around, there he was. He wasn't close, mind you, mostly he was a dark shape, but he was still *there*.

It sent a streak of irritation through me, and I sped up my pace, going over needlessly difficult terrain. Let's see him keep this up for long!

I lost him quick enough and felt a fierce satisfaction.

Then night came, and out in the distance I saw the tiny little flicker of a fire. Annoyance surged through me again.

I got up early, before the blue had been burned away by gold, and set off. I went fast, zigzagging and crossing my tracks and making it as confusing as possible as I headed north. At least I hadn't told him my destination.

By midday, I was confident he would have lost my trail. I went more leisurely, shooting a rabbit and roasting it for a good meal. Behorra almost burned her nose on the fire. She was getting too curious for her own good.

Come nightfall, there was once more a fire in the distance.

I aggressively sharpened my knife until the light was too dark, and then I had nothing to take my feelings out on. He was still following me! How dare he still follow me! How did he even *manage* to keep following me?

I hardly slept, determined to outpace him and leave him far, far behind the next day.

I made a point of wasting time leaving an obvious trail heading west, then went back to my heading of north. I even got some good distance in, because I coaxed Behorra into letting me ride her at a bouncy trot for a while.

I walked for a while, even well into sunset, feeling confident that, finally, I must have lost him. I settled down, pleased with myself.

When I woke up, my nose was filled with the smell of the smoke of wet wood. I looked and saw him in the middle distance, lying down and sleeping as if dead to the world. His fire was more smoke and steam than flame. He must've walked all night.

"How's he doing it?" I asked Behorra. "And why is he so determined? He's just getting himself lost."

Behorra didn't have any answers. She seemed less concerned about him than I did. I sighed, my insides all tangled up and cross. I simply wasn't getting rid of him.

I was sick of wasting the time and energy trying to lose him. He wasn't going to be fooled, somehow, and the longer I spent wandering around, the worse the souls of my clan got. He could keep up this deranged attempt to keep following me, and I hoped he'd grow bored of it after a day or two more.

Though I left before he awoke, he quickly closed the distance between us. He wasn't close, exactly. I could see him, make out a few details, but one of us would have to shout to have even a chance of hearing the other. I expected him to start yelling at any moment, but he remained silent.

He just followed me at that distance. Like a shadow.

Frustration pulsed through me all the time. I didn't get why he was doing this. We didn't really know each other, nor did he get anything out of it. It just . . . made no sense.

I shot down a few birds one day, using some of their feathers to repair my arrows. As far as I could tell, my follower preferred using a spear to hunt over a bow. I could appreciate that.

I sighted down the arrow shaft, ensuring I got the spiral of the fletching just right. There was a tall stone with rings carved in the distance that was good for focusing on.

Wait a minute. I stopped bothering with the arrows and made my way over to the stone. It was tall and alone, and oddly rectangular with straight sides. As I got closer, shapes and symbols began to appear on its surface.

They were worn smooth by rain and crusted with lichen, but I could still make them out. A set of concentric rings, the shapes of people, and the signs we used for certain constellations as well as for a sacred place.

Just as my father had described to me, here were directions to the place I sought. Or at least to the next marking stone. I thought there were several such stones, all over the place, and I didn't know which one in the chain this would be.

I committed the marks to memory. I wondered what it had been like, to be one of my ancestors, leaving a place so important they had to leave a permanent trail to find it again. My ancestors got to do all the impressive, important things.

I was just a wanderer followed by a horse and a weird guy. That felt like a pretty good omen I wasn't destined for anything much.

I followed my new heading the next day, the hunter once more just on the edge of a creepy distance behind me. It was annoying how I couldn't lose him. When he was behind me it felt like I had an itch on the back of my neck.

We kept walking for a few days. The weather was warm and pleasant, with the sun bright and the sky clear. The bugs were starting to come out in full force, and the animals were all beginning to have their babies. Young were easy prey, but it wasn't good practice to hunt them.

Behorra found a good, lush field full of the leafy grasses she favoured. It was close to a large copse of trees, something almost big enough to be considered a forest, which had several trees that put out spring nuts.

Nuts were always a welcome addition to my food stores, so I left Behorra to her meal and ventured in. The ground under the trees was uneven and sloped upwards, but the going was easy enough. I soon filled a pouch with nuts and started on a second one.

A gentle rushing sound played on the edge of my hearing. I made my way towards it, for loud river streams always ran clear and sweet.

The river, a fast moving thing, had cut through the land, a deep, curving scar rushing beneath me. I stared down at the white froth. I wouldn't be collecting any of that water. The steep slope down to it was covered in rich, healthy greens.

It was a veritable feast, in a sense, and they would keep fairly well. The ground wasn't that steep near the top, either, I thought, and it wasn't like I was going to try going anywhere near the river's depth.

I set my things down at the base of a tree and set my feet on the slope. It held well, and it didn't take much effort to balance on it. I stepped along it and crouched down to start cutting.

It didn't take long to fill up a pouch and tie it to my belt. The cut ends were releasing a fragrant smell. I reached out to gather another handful.

The world around me began to tilt, and I could hear the clatter of dirt and stone and my foot was trying to catch itself on air. My heart stopped. My breath hitched.

No, *no, no* – My thoughts spiraled.

Shock jolted through my arm and shoulder, a hard snap traveling through me. I blinked and looked up.

Kemen, the hunter from the marsh, had grabbed my wrist, his other hand gripping the trunk of a sapling. He was breathing hard. I was, too. My body was precariously sprawled on the steep slope, feet dangling over the raging water below.

I didn't want to fall.

I reached up with my other hand and grabbed his arm.

His muscles strained as he pulled me up. My feet scrambled against the slope, toes digging in wherever they could. I held on so tight my knuckles were white.

My feet reached the top of the embankment. Kemen reeled back, giving a final, sharp tug, and I found my weight tipped forward.

The two of us crashed into the ground, him beneath me.

My heart hammered and I struggled to remember how to breathe. His face was *right there* and I wasn't falling to my death. There was a speckling of freckles on his nose and his eyes had hints of dark blue.

His hand moved, half lifting towards one of the braids falling over my temple.

I pushed myself off him and scrambled back. I marched away from the edge, something in me shuddering.

I heard him sit up and paused. "Thank you," I said softly over my shoulder. I rushed back through the trees and out into the grasses where Behorra still ate. I buried my face in her mane for just a minute.

That was all the indulgence I would give myself.

I made a cheery, roaring fire that night. I wanted to feel safe and grounded and the heat of the fire settled a little bit of warmth in my bones. Behorra lay down, not too near, not too far, and gave a great sigh as she warmed and settled to sleep.

I heard the crunch of footsteps, but I focused on throwing another branch on the fire. It crackled and sent up a wave of sparks. The shadow of Kemen appeared in the darkness of the rest of the world.

"Hi," he said.

I made a quiet sound in my throat. He came and sat down by the fire, stretching out his hands towards its flames.

"I wanted to make sure you were okay." He glanced at me, once and then away. "That was a pretty close call earlier, and memory serves you're not the *best* self-healer."

"I'm fine. I didn't get hurt," I said.

"That's good. I'm fine too, by the way, thanks for asking. Am I entitled to a cut of your harvest? You picked my favourite and I did save your life."

I flashed him an annoyed look, then made a big show about pulling out the bag, transferring two handfuls to another pouch, and tossing it over to him.

He gave a smile. "Thanks. You seem way better at foraging and hunting than me. I mean, I'm not bad, but I don't bring in enough to keep myself alive for weeks and weeks. It's pretty impressive that you can."

"It's not hard."

"Guess you're just talented, then. That's lucky. I've always had to work hard to be even halfway decent."

"I worked hard too!" I snapped. I swallowed down other words. "Forget it. It's been a long day; I'm going to rest."

I lay down on my back, feet towards the fire, fur coat over my chest, eyes towards the stars. There were so many stars.

"Oh, yeah, you're right. It has been a day. I should probably turn in, too." I heard sounds of him shuffling and settling. "You don't find it scary, sleeping with no one to watch the night? It freaks me out a little, to be honest. Or does your horse keep watch? Your horse sleeps, right? Seems to be a very unusual horse, after all . . ."

"Behorra sleeps," I said. "But she wakes easily. And she's loud."

"Like a dog?"

"Better than a dog."

"Mm, yeah, she definitely seems more useful than a dog." More shuffling sounds. "How'd you . . . I mean, horses are wild, but she's not. It just – seems impossible. Especially since she's not a demon."

". . . I shot her," I began. I heard him shift eagerly and cleared my throat. "After that I'm not really sure how. It just happened. But now there's me and her and that's enough."

"Is it?"

I didn't bother to give that a response. Kemen shifted again. "Hey, can I come a little closer? I'm used to sharing a pallet with others, so honestly the past few nights I've been pretty sleepless and anxious."

"Do what you want."

On the edge of my vision I saw him get up. I figured he'd move more towards the fire by my feet, but instead he lay down next to me – *right* next to me. He was so close the hairs on my arm almost prickled from the proximity. The feeling made things inside me twist and bend.

"That's better," he said. "It's nice to feel less alone, don't you think?"

"I'm not alone."

"Right. You said that before. I suppose you have a good point, you have your horse. Me, though, this is the first time I've camped alone. It is not my favourite experience."

"You didn't choose that, when you had your coming-of-age ceremony?"

"Oh, no, I did go and survive alone for that, but, I mean, that's different. You know people are watching the area and keeping an eye out in case anything happens to you. Out here, you're just alone. No help is coming. That's what freaks me out."

"Well that's you."

"You really aren't very talkative, are you? Hey, do you at least remember my name?"

"Yes. It's Kemen."

"So you do remember! That's good. I honestly thought you'd forgotten." For a blessed moment, quiet fell. "Look, I know you're going through . . . a lot, and you probably want nothing to do with me, but I can't help but think you need someone on your side. And there doesn't seem to be anyone else offering."

"Be –"

"I mean a *human* on your side. A horse can't replace a human, not fully."

"Think what you want. It doesn't matter to me."

"You say that, but I . . . I can't wrap my head around it."

A bolt of tension shot through me. I was intensely aware of my hand, and his hand creeping close enough to touch.

I yanked mine away. "Don't do that," I snapped. It felt like my side was facing the fire, instead of my feet, and I didn't like it.

"Hm? Oh, sorry. I hadn't realized." An awkward beat fell as he shifted. "Do the Bizkor Oiloa know the same stories of the constellations as the Oin Zuria?"

"How would I know?" I settled myself into a position more comfortable and twisted my head so I looked away.

"What about the one, about the hunter and the fire bird?"

"I know it."

"Alright, do you want to tell it, then?"

"Why don't we just sleep?"

"Everyone knows you get a better sleep after sharing a story."

I made a vague sound that was almost a laugh in response to that.

"I'll tell it, if you don't want to.

"Long ago, many demons walked the earth, from the behemoths whose bones we still build our homes from, to strange spirits who could drive you mad with a glimpse. There were no clans in those days, for there were few humans and they stayed with their blood families, hiding in crevices to protect them from everything. One of these humans was a man named Gaizka, who protected his family by night, and hunted game by day.

"One day, Gaizka was on the trail of a behemoth, spears in hand, but by the time he had brought down the beast, he realized the day had grown late and he had strayed far from his family. As the night is a dangerous time, he sought out a place of safety for the night. It fell dark before he could find such a place, but in that darkness, he saw something.

"It was as bright as the sun, but smaller, and it flitted through the night sky with an orange glow. Drawn to it, Gaizka followed the strange light. When he grew close he discovered – the thing was a bird! A bird whose feathers were made of light and whose flight was made of heat.

"No sooner did he realize this, did the bird vanish, and the morning sun rose."

I was hardly listening. I knew this tale, and I tried to focus my ears on the sounds of the night, not his voice.

"Gaizka returned to his family and told them what he saw. They thought he had dreamed it. Gaizka was determined to prove to his family that the strange bird existed. He bid them goodbye, took with him his spears, and went to seek out the bird.

"During the day, he saw not a single feather. When night fell, he would see the glowing bird dance in the sky. He followed it for so many days, they became moons, and Gaizka became thin from lack of eating."

My hand prickled again, Kemen's hand creeping closer and closer.

"One night, the strange bird rested. It settled itself atop a rocky hill and tucked its head under its wing. Gaizka took the opportunity to sneak up on it."

A little bit of tension thrummed through me. Kemen's fingers moved just a bit against the back of my hand.

"The bird was even more wonderous up close. Its feathers crackled and glowed, bright as the sun and as warm as sunlight. Its heat went right to Gaizka's bones."

I tried to focus on anything, even his stupid story, to not pay attention to the feather-light feel of him stroking the back of my hand.

"Gaizka wanted to show his family this wonderous creature, and as a hunter he only knew one way, so he readied his spear to strike. But before he could drive the point home, the bird awoke and flew away into the dawn in a flurry of sparks.

"Disappointed, Gaizka returned to hunting the bird. How could he return home, without this incredible prize to show his family? More moons passed, and those moons became years."

What I wanted to know, was why he kept moving his fingers against my hand.

"Eventually, Gaizka's strength failed him. His legs could no longer run, his arms could no longer lift his spear, and his eyes could see little besides the brightness of the bird. He fell to the ground, wishing he could at least see his family one last time.

"That winter night, as Gaizka lay there, the bird approached him. It flew above him in the air, but Gaizka did not rise to chase it. As dawn approached, the bird landed next to Gaizka, who gathered the strength to raise his hand, hoping, perhaps, he could at least touch the bird before he passed.

"The bird did not want to be touched, but it admired the man who had played with it for so long. So the bird went over to Gaizka's ear and in it whispered its song, and through its song, strength and knowledge flowed through Gaizka. The bird then curled itself around the end of the man's spear, and then, when the spear itself glowed bright, it took off.

"With the fire on his spear to light the way, and the fire bird's knowledge of how to create it inside him, Gaizka made the long journey back to his home. His partner was long dead, but his children lived on, and their children as well. They were in awe of his fire, and he showed them how to make it.

"With the fire, Gaizka and his family had no need to fear the night. Fire warmed the body and heart and kept evil at bay. To thank the fire bird for its gift, Gaizka and his family decided to share it, and they set out to find other blood families, and teach them the secret of fire.

"Eventually came the day when Gaizka died, but on that day, something wondrous happened. All those who were present were amazed that, when night fell, the fire bird appeared. It landed on Gaizka's chest, and the two of them turned into a shower of sparks. The sparks flew high, so high that they settled among the stars, and there they remain to this day, an eternal game of tag, watching over the world below."

The snap of the fire seemed fitting in the silence that fell.

I drew in a shuddering breath. "Why did you pick that story?" I asked.

"I don't know," he said after a moment. "Maybe it reminded me of you. Did I tell it well?"

His finger brushed the back of my hand again. "Well enough."

The quiet stretched out, a tenuous, coiling thing in the night. Behorra's slow breathing calmed my heart. I fixed my gaze on the far-off, dark horizon. The stars were blazing above.

"Ainara."

"What?"

"Ainara. It's my name."

A slow exhale. "It's nice to finally meet you, Ainara."

I told myself that the sound of my name did not send a longing thrill through me.

CHAPTER 7
TEARS TO FILL A LAKE

I AWOKE TO AN offering of porridge, which was a nice
surprise. Behorra was already up and chomping on grass,
and the warm meal set a heat in me that I could feel down to
my toes. Kemen had several tools handy for cooking, but just
the fact I didn't have to stoke the fire and figure out what I
was doing was nice.

As I packed up from the night, Behorra trotted over and
away, over and away.

Kemen studied her. "What's she doing?"

"You're confusing her," I said. "Here."

I grabbed his wrist and led the way over to Behorra. She
snorted and stamped at the ground. I held Kemen's hand out
and put some of her favourite grasses in his palm. "Come on,"
I said to her.

She cautiously stepped closer, stretching out her head and
neck. Her lips flapped as she tried to eat without touching
Kemen. The expression on Kemen's face – all big eyes –
almost made me laugh.

Having had her treat, Behorra sniffed Kemen's hand, then
my hand on his wrist, then decided to bat at both our hands
with her nose. I gave her a pat on the neck. "See, he's not
really scary," I said to her.

"I think Behorra's the one who's scary," Kemen said. "Or maybe both of you."

I rolled my eyes. "She's just a horse."

"I know. You've been very clear on that."

"I don't want you trying to eat her again."

"I'm not going to eat her!" He cleared his throat. "So where exactly are you headed, anyways? I take it you're not just wandering around aimlessly."

"I said I found a sacred arrow. So I am going to check one of the sacred spots."

"One – you know the way to a sacred spot?"

"Yes – why do you look so surprised?" I asked.

He studied Behorra. "In the Oin Zuria, being told how to find the path to sacred spots is considered a great honour."

"Oh." I shifted my weight. "I never thought of it like that. It was just part of my aita's teachings."

"I see." He straightened up. "So, which way do we go?"

I pointed north-northeast. "I'm not sure of the distance, mind you."

"I'm sure it can't be too far."

I didn't know how many days walk he thought it might be, but whatever it was, it was too low. We walked for three days, and by the third day he was visibly frustrated, though he didn't say anything.

I felt we were making good time, for we went at an easy pace and hunted as we went. The closer we got, the more marked stones with directions there were. The carvings weren't always the easiest to read, but spotting the stones gave me a great sense of calm and stability.

My people were gone, but at least we had left a mark on the world.

We came to the top of a hill, and in the distance it glimmered. Kemen gave a low whistle. "Yeah, okay, it's breathtaking," he said.

"Yes, it is," I agreed, and started down the hill.

The lake was large, a great, shining thing stretching almost from horizon to horizon, its shore sand and smooth pebbles. Out in the middle of it was a sandy island, on which a small grove of trees grew. Cairns lined the perimeter, covered in flaking ochre. The water was blue and smooth.

I peered into the shallows, startled at how clear it was. I could see all the stones in the lakebed, and the small, dark fish darting about.

"It seems quite shallow," I said, crouching on a rock at a curve in the shoreline. I reached down and swished my fingers through the clear water. "It's warm, too."

"Is it?" Kemen dipped his hand in. "You're right, it's quite nice. It's been a while since I've come across water this warm. Actually, it's been a while since I've used water for anything other than drinking and cooking, now that I think of it."

I pinched at my clothes. "You have a point." I eyed the island with its tree. "I mean, really it's the *trees* that are sacred, not the lake itself . . ."

Kemen flashed me a grin. "I like the way you think."

While Behorra took a long drink and splashed a little, Kemen and I dropped our gear and supplies and found spots along the shore. I wasted no time in stripping off my clothes and wading in until the water reached my chest. The warm water was soothing on my skin.

I ducked my head beneath the surface, the water making an echoing roar in my ears, and scrubbed my hands through my hair. My scalp felt so tight and mucky I immediately wanted to redo my hair.

I spent a few minutes rinsing grime and sweat off of me. It made me feel light and relaxed. I'd forgotten if some spots on my arms were freckles or dirt.

Feeling much more like a human again, I splashed out to the shallows and sat down. It was painstaking, to undo my braids and let my hair fall in wet, tangled clumps. I carefully set my bead strands on the shore to dry. They were one of the last things I had from my family, as proof of who I was.

My fingers raked through my hair as I undid the wet strands, snarls making me wince. It'd been a long time since I'd had my hair unbraided, and the hairs tickled me as the wind blew it out like a curtain.

Once the worst of the knots were out and the things stuck in it were gone and the wind had dried it almost completely, I started the task of braiding. It turned out, it was a lot harder to do it on your own head, than on someone else's.

I heard footsteps on the rocks. "Ainara? I don't suppose I could get your help?"

I stood up and waded onto shore, stepping carefully over to where Kemen stood. He was still dripping, and was flapping out his wet clothes to lay them on a rock in the sun. His dark hair fell around his face boyishly.

He glanced over at me. "Looks like I'm not the only one who can't braid their own hair."

". . . Normally ama and Eider and I do it for each other," I admitted.

"It's my aita usually, for me. You want me to do your hair? I've been doing it for my younger sisters and cousins for years."

"Sure."

I brushed off the rocks and sat down, feet in the shallows. After a moment of hesitation, I handed Kemen my bead strands.

Kemen crouched down behind me and I tensed a little when he took my hair in his hands.

He worked quickly, his fingers gentle and deft. The clack of my bead strands as he wove them in carried with it memories. Lots of memories.

He knotted the braids off. "Done," he said. "Does it feel okay?"

I tilted my head side to side, feeling the weight as it shifted and swung. He'd bound all the braids into some complicated fall at the back of my head, but it didn't tug.

"Yeah," I said, standing up. "I'll do yours now, if you want."

Kemen blinked, then smiled. "Sure."

He seated himself and I knelt down behind him. There were scars, scratches from something, on the back of his shoulder.

I took a moment to trim the ends with my knife and spread his bead strands out next to me. The bits of shell and bone were coloured and ordered differently than the way we did it in my clan.

Kemen's hair was thick and prone to curling, which made it a bit difficult to work with. It seemed to take me far longer than he had to do the braids, and he had shorter hair than I did. I couldn't help but think, as I wove the bead strands in, that the contrast between their colour and his hair was striking.

"There you go," I said, leaning back.

Kemen brushed a hand through his new braids and grinned at me over his shoulder. "Thanks."

I stood up and rolled my shoulder. "No big deal. Having a bit of a break wasn't . . . bad."

"And now it's back to sacred arrows and vanishing clans," Kemen sighed. "You think it's possible to swim out to the island?"

I gauged the distance. ". . . No."

"– Can the horse swim it?"

"I don't want to find out in case the answer's no."

"Fair enough. Well, maybe there's a boat hidden somewhere, or a secret path to cross to the island. We ought to start looking."

"You can start looking," I said. "I'm putting my boots and clothes on first." The breeze, though slight and summer warm, was enough to chill me when I was still slightly damp.

I got dressed quickly, while Kemen shrugged on his still wet first layer and began walking along the shore.

Behorra was taking advantage of the good bath water, so I left her to enjoy herself while I found a good, long stick, and used it to poke about in the shallows. Even though the bottom had sandy patches, it still seemed fairly solid. No hidden paths just below the surface yet.

"I'm not seeing anywhere to hide a boat," Kemen said, tromping back towards me. "It's all pretty flat and exposed. Any luck?"

"None yet," I said. I frowned at the lake. "Is it just me, or does it seem darker over there?"

Kemen looked at the water. "It does . . . but deep water doesn't help us."

"Maybe, but – it's odd it's only darker and deep right there, isn't it?"

I waded out towards the dark patch of water, testing the ground in from of me with my stick. The water sloshed up to my knees, and then the stick met with no resistance.

I nearly lost my balance and dropped the stick. I backstepped, then frowned at the clear water. "There's a really sudden drop here. Like. A pit."

"A pit?" Kemen waded out to join me. "Yeah, this doesn't look normal. It's like someone dug a big hole. – This is a sacred place, so we're not staring at the way to the world of demons, are we?"

"I don't know." I squinted at the water. "Is – what am I seeing, there, on that shelf?"

Kemen dropped to his knees to get a better look. "That doesn't look like a plant. Or a fish. Maybe a turtle?"

"It's not moving."

"I'm trying to think of non-demon options."

"Well, there's one way to find out."

Before Kemen could properly protest, I took a big gulp of air and jumped off the edge.

The water was cooler here, and seemed to push against me as I dived. Swimming always gave me a strange feeling – my heartbeat in my ears, how light my limbs were – that I imagined was similar to being an otherworldly presence.

My hand closed around the strange object, many edges poking sharply into my flesh. I kicked for the surface.

My head broke into the air and I gave a great, shuddering cough as I treaded water. Kemen, face white with anxiety, leaned forward to offer me his hand. I paddled over and took it, letting him pull me to where the water wasn't deep.

"How 'bout you *don't* do that again," he said.

"It's effective."

"I'm wondering how you're still alive."

"I'm determined to not die. That's how."

"Terrible excuse. Let's go back to shore."

Kemen practically dragged me out of the lake, back to where Behorra and our things were. Behorra had moved on to finding whatever few bits of grass she could. Kemen sat down on the ground. "Right. So what did you find?"

I set between us something wrapped in a scrapped skin, which was ripping. I cut the bit of sinew holding it closed and its contents spilled in front of us.

Bead strands.

Long, sinuous strands of shell, shell, bone, stone, bone, horn, repeating after one another, fine patterns inscribed and dyed with ochre. The same patterns worn in my own hair.

I felt like I couldn't breathe, like my chest was consumed by that crushing feeling until my lungs had ceased to exist. My fingers trembled as they reached out to pick up a strand. I could hardly feel it, but it was real.

"This can't be right." I could hear my voice, but it was like another was speaking through me. I was on my feet, since when was I on my feet? I wanted to fly away, no, I wanted to be swallowed by the earth.

"That's from your clan, isn't it?" Kemen asked.

"Of course it's from my clan!"

The strand was bright in my hand, bright and pale and wrong.

"It was only put there recently, judging by the colours. So how did –"

"Because someone took it! Because a *human* KILLED them, don't you get it?" I flung my hand out towards the lake, the bead strand swinging like a talisman. "If a demon had been the one to drag them into the lake, there wouldn't *be* anything left – or if there was, it'd be a hand or a head or – not *this!*" I shook the bead strand in his face. "Things like this – they only have meaning for humans! Only humans think – only humans *know* – this is part of a person!"

My knees gave out. The bead strand fell from numb fingers. I couldn't breathe – I couldn't breathe – "They're dead. They're all dead. Everyone . . ."

My chest was being crushed into nothing. My throat closed up and burned along with my eyes and nose.

There was a horrible sound ringing through the air. A sound to tear your heart and mind to shreds. Everything around me blurred and burned.

Something warm and solid snaked around me, a boundary between where I ended and the crushing began. There was familiar yet unfamiliar touch, familiar yet unfamiliar words, something so right and so wrong because what was so right, was gone forever.

A great, strange hiccupping sound burst out of me, and then tears were running down my face, tracing over my nose, my lips, dropping off my chin in a horrible, ticklish feeling.

My throat burned and tore as I wailed, I couldn't get any air in, but I couldn't *stop*. The crushing feeling had crushed me so tight my insides were bursting out.

The horrible ringing sound faded to nothing. I felt like I'd been scoured to nothing and only numbness remained.

My breath still shuddered, and Kemen had stopped speaking, though he still held me tightly. My head rested on his chest, and I could hear his heartbeat, slow and steady. Gradually, I felt my own slow to match his.

My head felt strangely placed on my neck, but the rest of me had settled in my skin, and I pushed myself away from Kemen. ". . . I'm sorry," I managed hoarsely.

"You don't have anything to be sorry for," he said.

I scrubbed at my face with the heel of my palm. It came away wet. "I just . . ."

Kemen closed his hand over mine. "The dead like it when we mourn, for it reminds them of love and life. My only question is this: what are you going to do next?"

CHAPTER 8
THE HERD ENCOUNTERS THE HUNT

T HE FIRST THING I did, after calming Behorra, who'd run off in a fright and was hesitant to come back, was dig a grave. It wasn't a proper grave, for there was no House of the Dead, nor was there a body to lay out, but I was *not* leaving the bead strands in the lake.

I dug the grave by myself, neatly arranging the bead strands in the bottom. This time when I spoke the prayers, Kemen's voice echoed alongside mine. It gave the prayers a warmer feeling.

The day had grown late, so Kemen started a fire and caught some fish to roast. I wanted to help, to add a rabbit or duck, but my hands had begun to shake when I went to pick up my bow.

The smell of smoke and fish filled my nose and settled my nerves. Behorra gave a curious sniff and decided she didn't like fish.

"Do you have an answer?" Kemen asked, as the moon appeared in the pale sky.

"I want to find who did this. I want to know *why*. And I want them to pay," I said.

Kemen gave a slow nod. "Honestly, I still can barely wrap my head around it. I mean, this wasn't an accident. Someone, or a lot of someones, intentionally attacked your clan and – and killed everyone. Why . . . why would anyone do that? We're all humans, so how – how could they even bring themselves to do it?"

"I don't know. People fight, but the thought of intentionally *killing* another person – it makes me feel sick."

He threw a log on the fire. "Well, you found a sacred arrow. It seems we can't get to the island, but I think we both know who could."

". . . The Koba Altua." I leaned back. "The great peacemakers. They teach our seers and spirit walkers, they do so much to maintain the borders between the living, the dead, and the demons. Would they . . . really do this?"

"I don't know. It – it doesn't seem right. But they know the way to every sacred spot, how to properly use sacred materials. They may know more about the arrow," he said.

I fingered the fletching of the sacred arrow. "And if they're the ones behind this? What if they want me dead, too?"

"They wouldn't –" Kemen froze and frowned. "No, they might. You have a point. We don't know if or how they're connected, and if you show up out of nowhere, they might even think you've allied yourself with demons." He looked at Behorra. "I think the horse is going to cause you lots of problems."

"Well she's staying! Me and her – we're the only family the other's got anymore."

Kemen's face softened. "I know. I'm just saying, you're going to need help."

I exhaled. "Right. I – I suppose you're going to want to go home to your clan now –"

"Ainara." Kemen leaned across the fire. "I was talking about me."

". . . Oh."

He shook his head. "Did you really think I was going to abandon you now?"

"I don't know. I don't understand why you want to help me to begin with."

Kemen looked up at the moon. "I don't really know myself, either. Maybe it started because you were kind to a wild horse, and to a stranger stuck in a marsh. Now . . . I just want to. I don't think I'd forgive myself if I left you alone like this."

I didn't say anything, just let the quiet stretch out. I wasn't sure what to say to that, anyway.

I plucked a fish from the fire, even though I thought it wasn't quite cooked yet. "Whether they had a direct hand in this or not, we've only got one place to start. So how do we find the Koba Altua?" Kemen asked.

I took a bite of the fish. "Unlike most clans, they don't travel as far in the winter. They mainly stick to the same region, near a waterfall."

"Oh, right, the Flame Fall. You know, I thought that place was made-up when I was a kid. I still can't actually imagine a cave behind a waterfall that has a *fire* in it. Fires are things people make, not something that just – floats in a cave."

I nodded. "It did always strike me as weird, but what do I know about waterfalls and their spirits? The problem is, I don't know where the waterfall is. Ama once told me and

Eider it was to the east, so far to the east of where we camped, that even a stag could not run there. But that was years ago."

"Not the greatest set of starting directions," Kemen said, "but we have one thing going for us – instead of a stag, who cannot run that far, we have a horse."

"You don't seriously think Behorra can find it?"

"No. She'd need to be magical for that. But if she runs until she can't, then we'll have to be close."

"We're nowhere near where my clan camped when ama told me that! And even if Behorra *did* run in the right direction, we can't keep up with her."

"We don't have to keep up with her – I saw you sitting on her back as she ran."

I tossed some fishbones into the fire and gave Kemen a look. "Sure, I can ride her, but you?"

"How hard can it be?"

I nearly choked on my fish. "Okay, I'm going to enjoy tomorrow."

Kemen stuck his tongue out at me.

Come morning, Kemen was eager to try riding Behorra. He boasted that he'd ridden mouflon and aurochs all the time as a child. I fought the urge to laugh at the rude awakening he was about to get.

I called Behorra over to us and had her stand still. I stroked her face as I smirked at Kemen. "Go ahead," I told him.

Since Behorra no longer feared him, Kemen was able to walk right up to her and grab a fistful of her mane. His leg hit her in the rump as he swung it over, and the moment he sat down, she threw her head down.

Kemen slid down her neck and landed in the dirt at my feet. I crouched down and poked his forehead. "Still think it's easy?" I asked.

He looked at me from where he sprawled and spat out grit. "This was a stupid idea."

"Keep trying. Maybe next time she'll throw you in the lake."

"Very funny –"

A sacred arrow sprouted from the ground between us. I jerked back so fast I landed on my butt, and Kemen scrambled to his knees. "Uh, you didn't drop that, did you?" he asked.

I shook my head, my eyes already tracing back the arc the arrow must've taken.

Crouched in a crevice, some distance away, was a man.

I lunged for my bow, snatching it up. I yanked an arrow back on the string, but it shook so much when I sighted, I couldn't get a clear shot. I felt like I was going to throw up. The strange man started running.

I dropped my bow and vaulted onto Behorra's back, snapping, "Spear!" at Kemen, who already had one in hand. I tightly twisted my free hand into Behorra's mane and coaxed her after the man, hoping I wouldn't fall off. I'd never tried riding without both hands to hold on.

Behorra's thundering steps made the man turn pale and we caught up with him in seconds. I cracked the butt of the spear into his back as we tore past.

It took me some distance to get Behorra to slow and stop and turn around, so by the time she'd trotted back to where the man lay, Kemen was already sitting on his back, going through his things.

I slipped to the ground and planted the butt of the spear by the man's face.

He was a pale fellow, with a long nose and brown hair the colour of young wood. He was doing his best to glare at us, considering his face was in the ground.

"Why'd he shoot at us?" I asked.

The man squirmed. "You seek to defile the sacred grove by bringing demons there! You are traitors to hu –" Kemen whacked him in the back of the head.

"He's just spouting nonsense about demons. Behorra scared him."

"Aren't there horses around here?"

"I guess not her breed." Kemen pointed to the man's bow and arrows. "It's all made from sacred wood, though. And his supplies and stuff are fresh and maintained, there's gotta be an out camp in the area."

"Huh." I crouched down. "So which clan are you from?" I asked him.

He didn't say anything. I sighed. "Can we just strip him and throw him in the lake or something?"

"Do you have a nasty streak I don't know about?"

"Only to people who shoot arrows at me."

"Well, that's fair. I suppose we could take his food and leave him here. He'll know his way back to his out camp, so he should be fine –"

"Alright, alright! I'll tell you!"

I blinked in surprise. Kemen frowned down at the man. "I wasn't even trying to scare him."

"Maybe he can't breathe," I suggested.

"What is wrong with you two," the man muttered. "If I return having been sullied by a demon, it won't go over well for me. Only the strongest are allowed to aid in the mission."

"What mission?" I asked.

"Only the lady knows the specifics, but she assures us, it will save the world from ruin," he said.

Kemen raised an eyebrow. "Seriously? If you're going to talk, can you at least start from the beginning?"

"Only if you get off me."

I exchanged a look with Kemen. "He has a point."

Kemen pulled a face and slowly stood up. "Stab him if he tries to run."

The man pushed himself off the ground, rubbing at his ribs. He scowled at us, eyes roving over us. He went still as he looked at me, eyes widening slowly.

"What?" I demanded, not sure what about me horrified him so – it wasn't like there were any bloodstains, after washing in the lake.

"It's nothing," he said tersely. He cleared his throat. "For many years, I was without a clan – an accident led them to believe I had died, so I was separated from them. Some other clans would allow me to shelter as a trader for short times, and that was how I met the woman from the Koba Altua. At least, that's what she claims. I haven't met any of her clansmen. But she knows things, things only one who hears ancestors and spirits could know, so I believe she is what she says. She's a kind woman, offers a place for people like me, who don't have a home to go back to."

"That's good of her. People shouldn't be alone." Kemen flashed me a meaningful look.

I ignored it. As Kemen kept pointing out, any normal person would jump at the opportunity to be welcomed into a community after finding themselves adrift in the wild. I was a deranged unlikelihood for refusing. Still – that light in his eyes. The offer of a home seemed almost double-edged. "So then, why a mission, why give you sacred arrows? You haven't told us what you're doing here."

"I told you – I don't know exactly what the mission is, just that it's important. The lady gave some of us sacred arrows, because she said demons may try to interfere and we must stop them if they do. But she only has need for the best of us. If I return having been robbed, by someone with a demon, no less, I will no longer be of use to her. I will lose my home again."

Kemen leaned towards me and whispered, "Is it just me, or is this starting to sound a little messed up?"

"Okay, but why *here*, specifically," I pressed.

"Because this is where a sacred grove grows. It must be protected. We take turns coming out here, to ensure that all is still well. Today was my turn."

". . . How long have people been protecting this place?" Kemen asked.

"Uh, I believe the lady had us begin more frequent checks on sacred sites about a couple moons ago. Right after – some things." The man pressed his lips together.

A thread of tension crept through me. I didn't like that timing. It was all far too coincidental.

Kemen crossed his arms and looked at me. "I think we need to talk to this lady. It sounds like she's the only one who actually knows anything."

"You're right," I agreed. "Where do we go, so we can meet her?"

"I do not know where the lady is at this time."

"You're being extremely unhelpful," Kemen said. "Would someone in your out camp know?"

"Possibly."

I stood up. "Then I guess you're taking us to your out camp."

The man scowled. "Why would I do that?"

"Because I can chase you down on a horse. Watching you run away would actually be funny."

He eyed Behorra nervously. "Are you sure that thing is safe?"

"Perfectly." I flashed a wolfish smile. "As long as you don't get on my bad side."

The man seemed skeptical, and he kept looking at me like I was a ghost, but he didn't argue. He clearly had no problem with Kemen, so I didn't understand why I got such a response just by standing there. Because of Behorra? He spoke of the 'lady' with such reverence, it couldn't be he had a dislike of women.

Kemen kept an eye on the man while I packed everything up. With three people, one of whom we didn't trust with anything, we had a lot of gear. Behorra wasn't happy about it, but I fashioned some bags together and slung them over her back. It made her resemble an auroch a little, which I didn't like, but practicality took precedence.

The man was all shifty eyed and surly as we made him lead the way. I kept Kemen's spear in my hand. I'd packed my bow, and the man's bow, onto Behorra. I couldn't trust my hands not to shake again.

We walked for a full day, the ground changing from low mounds of stone to something steeper, more jagged. The trees that grew were tall and thick-limbed, with dark leaves and prickly needles. It was a place where mist would easily cling.

About mid-morning, a thin, twisting column of smoke was visible, rising between the tree trunks.

"That's the out camp I was stationed at," the man said. "They won't take kindly to the two of you."

"They won't take kindly to Behorra," Kemen corrected. He shifted his weight, frowning. "Ainara, can you tie a rope around her, or something? Maybe we won't be filled with arrows if they think we captured a demon or something."

"She's not a demon," I grumbled; but I pulled out a coil of rope from Kemen's gear and tied a loop around Behorra's neck. She kept trying to chew on it until I swatted her nose away. I held the other end in my hand, the rope loose.

The man was still looking at me like I was some kind of spirit, like something that was wrong. Kemen seemed satisfied with the rope, even if I and Behorra weren't.

"Let's get this nightmare over with," the man said. Kemen shoved him forward and the man led the way down the path through the trees.

The closer we got, the more I could smell smoke and sweat. Behorra's ears were pricked up, flicking around, and she was taking choppy steps. The trees made all sounds muffled, turning voices into indistinct murmurs.

The man shouted a greeting, which made Behorra snort in surprise. Someone shouted back, and I noticed Kemen's hand on his knife. He shot an anxious look back at me.

The out camp was a well-established thing, with three huts of well-tanned skins and wooden frames, a stone-lined fire pit, and a woodshed for storing food and firewood. Two men stood by the fire with wide, staring eyes. I looked, but I didn't see another set of sacred arrows and bow.

"You're late," one of the strangers said. "Wait – who are . . ."

The other lunged for a spear.

"We're not here to fight!" Kemen shouted. "We just have a few things we want to know."

The spear was still pointed at us. "Identify yourselves."

"I'm Kemen, of the Oin Zuria. This is Ainara, and, uh, Behorra, of the Bizkor Oiloa."

There was a shift, a small, subtle thing amongst the strangers, and my nerves burned at it.

"How do you have a Zaldi?"

"It's a long story," I said. "But that's not why we're here. We want to speak with this lady you've been working with."

The men blinked. "You mean *the* lady? Why?"

"That's our business. We just want to talk to her. Do either of you know where she is?"

The three strange men exchanged looks and it seemed to speak volumes. Something about it set an uncomfortable itch between my shoulder blades.

The spear pointed at us was lowered. "You're in luck. The lady visited this camp a few days ago. She wanted to perform a ceremony of protection at a lake. She's headed southeast now, following the stars of the great river. Beyond that, we can't say."

"Did she give you a specific destination?" I asked.

"The lady doesn't tell the likes of us that kind of thing."

I made a face at that. What kind of person didn't tell others where they were going and what they were doing? Keeping those sorts of things to oneself – it was like this woman was asking for the world to kill her.

Behorra lipped at some leaves on a branch, and the three strange men flinched. I stroked the side of her neck, trying to put a name to the uncomfortable feeling that the way they looked at me caused. I couldn't.

Kemen stepped towards them. "You can't expect us to believe that –"

I placed my hand on his arm. He looked back angrily and I shook my head. Instinct told me something about all this was very wrong, and to get very far away. Kemen's expression mellowed a little, and he gave a tiny nod.

"Thank you for the information. We'll be going now," I said.

I tugged Behorra's face away.

"Hang on," said the man. "What about my equipment? You can't keep it!"

"We won't," I said. "You'll just have to find it tomorrow. Don't worry, I'll make it obvious."

The men gaped at me angrily, but I didn't care. I just wanted to leave.

I led the way through the woods, taking the rope off Behorra once the out camp was definitely beyond sight and hearing. She tossed her head happily at its removal.

I hopped over a snarl of tree roots. Kemen brushed a branch out of his way. "Do you really think this woman is the one behind what happened to your clan?"

"The timing lines up, and the sacred arrows, and . . . didn't you see how they looked at me?"

"I saw how they looked at Behorra, but that was expected."

I fought a shiver. "It was like I was – wrong."

"I'm sure you imagined it. But I agree that this woman probably knows something about what happened." He plucked a few early seeds off a branch and popped them in his mouth. "You think you can find her?"

"Why me?"

"Because you are obviously the more wood-savvy of the two of us. Actually, I think you're more capable than me in general," he said.

A tiny corner of my chest warmed. "Well, southeast following the great river is pretty broad, but since we're starting from the same place, we have a good chance of coming across her trail."

"Then we better not waste any more time."

We walked for quite a while after that. There were plenty of greens and meat to eat underneath all the trees, though the groves thickened and thinned as the ground rolled up and down. In the distance, I could see a tall slope covered in trees.

There were paths through the trees, places where feet had worn the dirt bare and bodies had broken back branches. They made it easy for Kemen and I to walk, and Behorra plodded along behind us, seeming to find the intertwining limbs of shrubs and saplings too much of a bother.

It was a bit comforting, that this area was so well traveled. It meant there weren't wolves in the area, and bears and boars would be few and far between. The eyes that I felt were watching me were imaginary; or from something not quite of this world.

I chose to believe it was the former.

When the stars came out, the great river blazed in the sky above us, blues and purples and greens and whites speckling and twirling together in a beautiful riot. It was so vivid here; it took my breath away.

Kemen leaned back to gaze up at it. "Sometimes I wonder if we can ever live up to our ancestors. I mean, they were around to see things like *this* be created. What can we do that could ever compare?"

"I think not dying is a good place to start. A lot of stuff exists because people died. I think, between creating a miracle and living, they would have preferred to live."

Kemen didn't reply to that. He just continued to look at the stars while I roasted some game in the coals. All I could think about, was that my people were all dead, and nothing had come out of that. Where were their constellations, or great trees, or springs?

Why did they all have to die, and the world had to continue on like nothing had changed?

Something had to come out of this tragedy. Something.

Chapter 9
The Hunter Commits Slaughter

U NDER THE BRIGHT YELLOW sun and the blue sky but in the shadow of the mountain, the trees filled with mists. It was a thin, smoky thing that carried with it the smell of water. It made shapes blur and smudge and shimmer like ghosts. Sounds had a strange, muffled quality.

Behorra stopped, ears pricked forward, her skin twitching and her tail swishing. I ran a comforting hand along her neck, wondering what it was that had startled her, when I heard it.

It was a woman singing.

The words were indistinct, like the words used in prayers that always sounded a little funny. It felt like the voice was rising up from the earth and trees and mist itself.

I caught the back of Kemen's clothes and mimed for quiet. His eyes widened as his ears caught the sound and he looked around. "Where's it coming from?" he whispered.

I pointed in the direction Behorra stared. "I'm going to say, that way."

The two of us walked softly towards the singing voice, its sound growing louder and more powerful. I caught a glimpse of slow, pale movement through the trees, gradually taking on the shape of a human figure.

Correction: revealing itself as a naked woman dancing.

That wasn't something one normally saw, especially not in the woods far away from a clan settlement. It made me wonder if I was imagining it.

Kemen slipped through the trees to a smallish clearing, where someone had recently left their gear, and now there was a woman singing and dancing. It looked like too many supplies to belong to the one woman alone.

"Uh, is she the person we're looking for?" Kemen asked me quietly.

"Let's ask." I stepped towards the woman and cleared my throat, waving my hand awkwardly. "Um, excuse me? Miss?"

The woman's voice faded away to nothing. She stared at me with large, limpid eyes that reminded me of a doe's. "Are you by any chance the, uh, the lady we've heard about? Um, how do I explain this . . ."

The woman laughed, a musical sound. "Oh, no, I'm not as gifted as her, though I'm flattered you believe so. Have you come to seek out her wisdom as well?"

"Sort of . . ."

"Well, she should be returning later. I'm just making sure no demons interrupt her – she is taking the sacrifice to the lake."

My insides ran cold. "Sacrifice?"

"Lake?" Kemen asked. "What lake?"

The woman pointed to the top of the mountain. "The lake up there. It is one of the last the receive its gift of a soul."

I tried to remember to breathe. "What – what are these sacrifices for?"

"For the waters. Nescato is completing the sacrifices to appease all the water spirits in the world. She is saving us from ruin."

"That's a . . . big undertaking," Kemen managed. He glanced up at the peak of the mountain. "Do you suppose she'd mind if we went up there and watched the, uh, ceremony?"

"Of course not!" Her smile turned dangerous. "She will gladly welcome those who can make it."

A chill had taken hold of my heart. "Come on," I said to Kemen, grabbing his arm. "Let's go."

We rejoined Behorra in the trees, and the woman resumed her singing, her song now taking on an eerie tone.

The trees thinned right near the base of the mountain, and I could see a path had been worn right around the peak, and that many trails seemed to be leading to this place from all directions. The mountain was a heavily wooded, misty place that seemed capable of hiding anything.

The broken pieces inside me jangled. I took the packs off Behorra and handed Kemen his things. "I don't want her burdened," I said.

Kemen nodded, and his eyes fell on my bow. "Are you going to be okay if you need to use that? The past few days . . ."

"I'll manage," I snapped, hating that he'd noticed the strange way my hands shook and my vision had blurred whenever I'd tried to shoot. If I didn't know better, I'd be worried some demon had possessed me.

There were a lot of bird songs as we ascended the mountain. The path was straight and sloping, though between the tree boughs and the mist, it was hard to see that far ahead.

Kemen suddenly stopped walking, then backed up until he was right in front of me. I made myself be more annoyed by that, rather than let myself think that his back was actually quite broad. I stood on my toes and peeked over his shoulder.

There were figures underneath the trees.

They'd painted their bodies with ochre and berries, and bones had been sewn along the edges of their clothes. Something about their eyes was – wrong. Fractured. I couldn't tell how many were men and how many were women, but I supposed it didn't matter.

They were passing a bird call along amongst themselves. Whatever bird they were mimicking sounded harsh and unfriendly.

Three of them raised bows and pointed the arrows at us.

It felt like the ground was pulled out from under me. Like the world around me was crumbling into something strange and hostile.

They were actually threatening to shoot us. People hunting people. And they were so calm about it.

Like they'd done this before.

I thought I was going to throw up.

Kemen pressed one of his spears into my hand. "If this turns bad, get on Behorra and run."

"What –" I hissed. Kemen stepped forward, head on a swivel as he gave people a stupid, fake smile. I resisted the urge to yank him into the trees and hide.

"We were hoping to meet Nescato," he said loudly. "What's with this hostility?"

"She's busy."

"Er, yes, we heard." Kemen took a couple more steps towards them. "But don't you think this is a bit much?"

Someone down the mountain copied the howl of a wolf. Behorra whinnied and skittered to the side, unable to tell the difference. She kicked a rock and spooked herself. "Behorra, no!" I cried, lunging for her.

People shouted oaths. Kemen yelled, "Don't!" and grappled with someone's aimed bow.

A pale, bone knife flashed by Kemen's side and he roared in pain.

"Kemen!" I shouted. His knee buckled under him.

"Go!"

"Stop her!"

I whistled and Behorra stilled enough for me to vault onto her. I gripped the spear tightly as I dug my heels in and clicked my tongue. She took off down the path, her body burning against the upward slope. Her eyes flicked every which way and she nickered nervously.

I glanced back, but I couldn't tell who was who, or if Kemen was alright. The forest and mist swiftly swallowed everything. My heart was pounding. Every part of me trembled.

As the forest closed around us, Behorra slowed. The way was getting steeper and rockier, tree roots exposed as their trunks clung to precarious purchases. I ran a hand along her neck, unsure if I was comforting her or myself.

Behorra's skin twitched and she arced her neck oddly. I murmured to her.

A fall of pebbles echoed and made both of us start. I watched as they tumbled away and forced my breathing to slow. I went to push Behorra forward again and more pebbles fell. I looked up their path.

A pair of feet were on the edge of the ridge, and those feet belonged to a woman who I knew instantly had to be her. Nescato.

She was a tall, curvy woman, with curled, brown-gold hair tied expertly back. A headdress of antlers and boar tusks made her shadow long and twisted. Over her clothes she wore an adornment on her chest that, if I didn't know better, I would've thought was made of human ribs. The bones were from a red deer's rib cage, tied together with sinew thread, and it gave her a discomforting, skeletal look. Her eyes – her eyes were pale in colour, but the fire in them burned hot and fierce.

In one hand she held a stone knife. In the other, she held a bead strand. A familiar patterned bead strand.

"You must be the reason for the alarm signals," she said.

It took me a try to get my voice to work, to get my words to sound even. "I have a question for you, Nescato. Are you the reason the Bizkor Oiloa are dead?"

She frowned prettily. "Now, why would someone like you know that?" Her eyes roved over me and landed on my waist. Her eyes widened. "Oh. I see. A survivor."

I almost asked how she could know, and then I realized – my father's atlatl. It was tied to my belt, so it was always close. And it was carved to resemble my clan's namesake, the stag.

"Answer me!" I demanded. "Did you kill my clan?"

She inspected the edge of her knife. "Well, not personally. I'm not much for hunting, you understand."

My insides were hot and cold. "Why?" My voice cracked. "Why did you kill everyone?"

She tilted her head, studying me, then nodded. "I suppose, considering the circumstances, it would be acceptable to tell you." She smiled at me. "I had wondered, if there were some unaccounted for. The souls did seem – restless. But I figured you'd blame demons and get killed by them, not tame one."

"Just tell me!"

"I'm getting to that. Be patient." She sighed. "This is the problem with outsiders. So rude."

"I'm only here because of you!"

"True. Well, a few moons ago, the ancestors had a very important message for me. A warning – a great disaster is about to strike, and we will all be at risk. In order to avert this, the world's waters must be appeased by an offering of great strength and sacrifice."

"So, you needed a large sacrifice and you – what? Chose people?"

She smiled a dazzling smile. "Exactly! I admit, my choice was – unconventional. Another of my clansmen would very likely have chosen aurochs, or even horses, like the one you're sitting on. But these sacrifices need to be *strong*. They will keep us all safe, after all. And we all know – it's humans who have the strongest spirits."

My hand tightened on the spear. "So that's the reason my people had to die? Had to be *slaughtered* like *animals*?"

She blinked, finally perceiving some of my anger. "Of course. Sacrifices must be properly prepared, and your clan was an excellent choice. Skilled, but small. Easily dealt with."

My whole body shook and my vision narrowed. "Why don't you come down here and say that to my face?"

"I'm not stupid, girl. I can safely deal with the problem from here."

"*Problem?*"

"Well, yes." She tapped the knife against her other hand. The sound of it striking the bead strands put my teeth on edge. "The spirits of the sacrifices have been . . . They've been fighting their bindings and refusing to do their new jobs. I didn't know why, at first, but now that you're here – they wish to join their last. The dead long for the living. The sacrifice is incomplete. As long as you live, they will be drawn to you."

"So you're going to kill me too?"

"Yes. You should be happy – with your death, the rest of us will be saved."

"Lady, if you think I'm going to sit here and let you kill me, you've got another thing coming," I growled.

"Oh. You're going to be difficult, I see. In that case –"

She pointed the knife tip to the sky.

I didn't stick around to find out what she had in mind. I urged Behorra forward, up the path, and she was all too happy to take off.

The figure of Nescato standing above me vanished behind the treetops, a frown on her pretty face. Behorra whinnied; I could feel it reverberate through me.

We took a corner on the path, the mountain top growing closer and flatter. The forest around us seemed to rustle, and the shadows in it looked like hunters.

Behorra slowed as the ground level out. The top of the mountain was an empty place, with a spring bubbling up to create a small lake, rivulets carrying the water to the world below. It was very green up here, so green it almost felt like a mockery.

On the shore was a firepit lined with stones, low flames tinged with ritual green. Laid out on the ground next to it were all the things needed for a sacrifice – herbs, garagarrd, ochre, a curved blade of shiny dark stone.

I dropped from Behorra's back, searching for any remains – I couldn't leave them in the hands of this woman. I sifted through the wood pile, the wood sticky with sap and something else.

Footsteps cracked something behind me. "Ah. So there you are."

I whirled around. Nescato smiled at me. "I've already burnt the bodies – corpses don't last long." She held up the bead strand looped and draping from her fingers. "This is all that's left, I'm afraid."

"Give it to me," I hissed.

"Dear girl – you won't need it where you're going."

She closed her hand around the strand and lifted the knife. I shifted into a crouch, scanning for the spot with the best cover for when the arrows came flying.

Nescato stepped calmly towards me. "Where are your friends who murder for you?" I growled.

She arched a delicate eyebrow. "You didn't think they came up here, did you? I'm performing a sacred ceremony – I can't have just anyone watching."

"Then who else is here?"

"Right now? No one. It's just you and me, and the ancestors."

"Good."

I lunged for her, tackling her by the waist. The knife flashed dangerously close to my eye. We hit the ground. Air rushed from me as her knee met my stomach.

She'd thrown the bead strand. I reached for it, and her hand closed around my hair and pulled. I screeched and scratched at her hand, grabbing her other wrist and holding the knife at bay.

Nescato cursed at me. I rammed my toes into her shin. She stumbled and I wrenched my hair free. I twisted and punched her in the face.

In that moment, I made a dive for the bead strands and my fingers caught the edge. I tugged it under me just before a weight hit my lower back.

I rolled and caught her hand with the knife pointed at my neck. "Stop fighting," she growled.

"Die yourself!" I hit her with the bead strands, cutting her cheek and temple, but hardly making her blink. I tried to hit her with my knees. She pressed the knife closer to me.

I reached with my free hand for something – anything – and my hand met something searing hot, but I didn't care. I threw the embers at her face.

Nescato yelped and flinched back. I pushed her away and shoved myself off the ground, not caring that my feet scrambled through the fire. Hot coals sprayed.

I needed some kind of weapon, something longer than a knife.

The spear.

I darted for it as smoke began to thicken in the air. Nescato was screaming foul words. A foot landed on my back, sending me sprawling.

I twisted and kicked my foot into her stomach. She doubled over and I kicked her again.

Flames were beginning to spread across the ground, plants catching.

Fire licked upon the bowl of garagarrd, and then it was all heat and flames and smoke and everything was burning.

Nescato screamed, "I'm trying to save us, you fool!"

I could just see her figure through the smoke and flames, coughing, looking.

I reached the spear and picked it up. Behorra was crying out, voice high with anxiety. Nescato turned towards her, knife raised high.

There was no time.

I ripped the atlatl from my waist and set the spear in. I barely sighted and threw it at Nescato's shadow.

She cried out, and I didn't stick around to see if she'd been fatally wounded. The air was thick with acrid smoke and the heat was uncomfortable on my skin. The flames reached the trees and spread fast.

I whistled, running for Behorra, and there she was, her eyes ringed in white. I snatched at her mane as she flew by and tumbled on.

She didn't need direction after that, tearing down the mountain path as fire chased her and smoke darkened the sky. I refused to look back as we flew down the mountain to the forest below.

Chapter 10
Tomorrow Carries the Scent of Freedom

FIRE STILL SPREAD ABOVE us, crackling and bright and powerful, but Behorra and I had slowed to a jouncing trot. I scanned the path for Nescato's friends, but the forest seemed abandoned.

Or perhaps they had run to Nescato's aid.

Behorra whinnied and a figure appeared on the path.

I didn't have a weapon. I goaded Behorra into a canter, hoping to race by them.

A bright grin and, "Thank the ancestors!"

"Kemen!" I exclaimed. I threw myself at him as Behorra thundered past and tackled him to the ground. "You're okay!" I grabbed him by the face and pressed my forehead to his. "I'm so glad you're okay."

Kemen's arms wrapped around my waist, pulling me tight against him. "Well, this is a nice reaction."

"Shut up."

"Make me." He moved his head, lips almost close enough to brush mine.

My heart rate stumbled and my mind buzzed and I moved back so I could think. "What happened?" I asked him.

He gave a lazy smile. "Honestly, once you got by, they panicked because they'd let a demon through and they scattered. I got a couple bruises and scrapes, but nothing serious."

I sat back, just in time for Behorra's return. She nosed at my shoulder and I patted her absently. "I had thought . . ."

"Hey, I'm more concerned about what happened to you. The mountain is now on *fire*. We should probably get out of here," he said.

I stood up. "Good point."

As the two of us walked through the woods, away from the mountain, I relayed to Kemen what Nescato had said about my clan and why they had to die and the oncoming disaster. I kept running the bead strand through my fingers. I couldn't tell whose, specifically, it had been, but it was one of my clan.

Its owner would be happier to be buried by me, I was sure. I wasn't about to let my clansmen's spirit be bound as some sort of guardian for eternity. I would find a good spot and bury it, and set them free.

I fell quiet at that thought. How many more of my people's bead strands had already been sacrificed to lakes and rivers? How many more had Nescato kept hidden away? What about all those souls? What would happen to them? Should I try to find who I could, and lay them to rest?

And what if Nescato wasn't dead? Or what if some of her friends knew the details of what she'd done – would they try to complete her mission? Would they come after me? Would I be safe . . . anywhere? How far did the reach of her mission extend?

Kemen reached out and slipped his hand in mine. "You okay? You look . . . I know what just happened was a lot, but, it's over now, isn't it?" He glanced back at the burning mountain behind us.

"I'm just . . . I don't know." I had too many questions, and not enough answers.

Kemen stopped walking and tightened his hand around mine. "Now that – now that we know what happened – Ainara, I still don't think you should be out here alone. I know before, you didn't feel like you could turn to anyone, but – I have a home. A clan. You could come back to them, with me. You could live with us. We –" His voice broke, and he gave me a sad sort of look. "I can already tell from your expression, the answer's no, isn't it?"

I lightly set my hand over his. "It's more complicated than that. I – I want Nescato to be dead, but I don't know. I don't know what happened to her. And what she did – taking my whole clan – she'd need more people than I can imagine to do that. More people than we've seen. She must be working with others, but until I know how far her reach is . . ."

Or, I thought, *until I know if anyone in your clan aided her.*

Kemen gave a soft sigh. "I understand. I think. We're suddenly dealing with something bigger and more complicated than I'd ever dreamed possible. If you're not ready, I won't push you. Just – let me give you directions to this year's settlement, and swing by the area every once in a while. Leave some sort of sign that you're doing okay, for me, alright?"

I gave him a small smile. "I think I can manage that."

"Good," he said, and gave my hand a squeeze.

We didn't part ways right away, for we were deep in the wilds, and we wanted to get a little closer to the place where the Oin Zuria lived, and where the Bizkor Oiloa had existed.

As the days passed, I found that Kemen's chatter could be quite comforting, that the crushing feeling was less often and less likely to squeeze me from existence, that the broken pieces inside me seemed to be knitting themselves back together. I missed all my people fiercely, but now I knew the reasons why, and for them – for my clan, I could live on.

On a bright and sunny afternoon, Kemen pointed out the haze and bumps in the distance that were his clan's settlement. It was larger than the Bizkor Oiloa's had been, and I could see well-minded herds and crops growing rich and lush. The Oin Zuria were a bountiful clan, it appeared.

I felt a little lonely at the thought that Kemen would be going one way and I another, but the thought of actually going to his clan made things unsettled inside me, and I was just starting to settle again.

Kemen was quiet as I memorized the landscape around his settlement. I wanted very much to be able to find my way back here.

"Are you going to be okay?" he asked.

"I should be asking that," I joked. "You left on pretty bad terms."

"Because of you!" He caught my hands. "Stay safe, will you? I don't want to hear a story about you and Behorra running into demon slayers."

"Then maybe you should start helping people realize that none of the horses from the east are Zaldi," I said.

"That . . . well, I can try."

After a moment's hesitation, Kemen pulled his second and last spear from his back. I'd lost his first one after throwing it at Nescato. He pressed the spear into my hands. "Keep this," he said. "For hunting, self-defence – whatever you need. It's a lot easier to use riding than a bow."

"Thanks." I'd have to figure out a good way to carry it, but for now I slipped it through the strap of my quiver. "And I'll come back. I promise."

Kemen gave me one more smile, and I climbed onto Behorra's back. I signaled goodbye with my hands and clucked my tongue at Behorra.

We rode away for a few minutes at a quick pace, because I was scared if we didn't, I'd turn us around. Behorra seemed to sense this, for she soon stopped and turned her head to look at me with her eye.

Last chance, she seemed to be saying.

I twisted around, looking back the way we'd come. Kemen was still standing there, a small figure, watching me. I sent him another goodbye, and this time he returned it.

I exhaled and leaned forward on Behorra's neck, breathing in her scent. "Where do you think we should go?" I asked her.

She shook out her mane and nickered.

I sat up. "You're right. Let's go everywhere."

Afterword

This story had been sitting in my heart for a while. It came from the fact that I love prehistoric fiction, but they only ever seemed to come in two varieties, and wanting something different I finally said, "screw it, I'll do it myself."

I want to thank my friends, who got a million Skype messages as I tried to figure out what was going to happen in the series. It was more helpful than I think they know. One of them also provided great advice when I was designing the cover.

I also want to thank the beta reader I found, "clooverhoover" [a screen name] for the invaluable advice given. And also the enthusiasm! I, too, greatly enjoy airheaded Kemen moments. It was so wonderful to know that someone read this and enjoyed it.

As to the historical accuracy of this story, that could likely cause anthropologists to debate until the cows come home. The setting is roughly 10,000 years ago, just before the Neolithic revolution has really caught on and spread, in the region of the border of what is now Ukraine and Belarus. I drew inspiration from the Neman culture in particular, though this story takes place earlier. I also drew a lot from archaeological sites further afield – there's limited resources for the specific time and region I'm writing about. I'm a mythology nut as well, so I definitely used that knowledge to flesh out the worldbuilding where I could.

The people at this time are what I have joking referred to as 'nomadic farmers' – though a more accurate term would be to say they are practicing a form of pastoralism. I came to this conclusion based upon what evidence I could find of their buildings and diet at this point in history. I'm sure, however, I got some of the details wrong. Maybe even intentionally! I do get creative license, you know.

There's no evidence for or against the domestication of horses at this time. The evidence we have for it doesn't provide a real origin point. As such, it is mostly based around a fictionalized event of when the family of horse breeds known as warmbloods came into existence.

I've had great fun writing this story, and in writing the sequels. The whole story has a ways to go, and *wow*, has the cast of characters gotten huge. I certainly hope you'll stay along for the ride, and enjoy it as much as I do.

Manufactured by Amazon.ca
Bolton, ON

39983912R00072